**You call *this* we~~~~~~~**

Marigold narrowed her eyes. "You do remember that I know witches and fairies and imps, all of whom could do you some harm if I asked them to."

"Are you threatening me?"

"Can you think of a reason why I shouldn't?"

Christian's pride prevented him from saying, "I'm sorry. I overreacted. I shouldn't have spoken to you the way I did." Instead, he unwisely said, "Do what you think you have to do."

She looked at him as if she didn't know him, then turned and left the terrace, with Flopsy, Mopsy, and Topsy at her heels. He watched her go with a chill around his heart. She *did* know witches and fairies and imps. But would she really use them against him? Didn't she love him enough not to do that? Didn't she love him at all? And how, in ten quick minutes, had they gone from a peaceful breakfast on the terrace to death threats? It was as if some toxic breeze had blown over them and poisoned the air they breathed, turning them into alternate versions of themselves, versions that were stupid and unpleasant and mean. They were acting like—like *Olympia.*

# Twice Upon a Marigold

## JEAN FERRIS

sandpiper

Houghton Mifflin Harcourt

Boston  New York

The inspiration for Mr. Lucasa's wonderful foreign words came from *The Meaning of Tingo: And Other Extraordinary Words from Around the World* by Adam Jacot de Boinod, to whom I offer my heartfelt thanks.

www.hmhbooks.com

Text set in Minister
Book design by Lydia D'moch

The Library of Congress has cataloged the hardcover edition as follows:
Ferris, Jean, 1939—.
Twice upon a Marigold/Jean Ferris.
p. cm.
Summary: After a quiet, happy year in a small town, Queen Olympia regains her memory and initiates new plots and manipulations, as the residents of Zandelphia and Beaurivage, now ruled by Christian, Marigold, and Swithbert, feel the effects of her bad energy.
[1. Fairy tales. 2. Kings, queens, rulers, etc.—Fiction. 3. Princesses—Fiction. 4. Amnesia—Fiction. 5. Trolls—Fiction. 6. Humorous stories.] I. Title.
PZ8.F387Twi 2008
[Fic]—dc22          2007035761

ISBN: 978-0-15-206382-5 hardcover
ISBN: 978-0-544-05098-3 paperback

Manufactured in the United States of America
DOC 10 9 8 7 6 5 4 3 2 1

4500397044

*For K.A.K., Gillian's prince charming*

# 1

The trouble began with the dogs: big, shaggy Bub and little, dramatic Cate; and the floor mops: Flopsy, Mopsy, and Topsy. They had lots of toys scattered all through the castle at Beaurivage, as well as at the crystal cave-castle, Zandelphia's royal residence across the river. There were chew toys, balls, flying toys, stuffed toys, toys on wheels, but there was just one blue squeaky toy. And that was the one they all wanted to play with.

When they were at the castle where the blue squeaky toy wasn't, they made do with what was available. But even when they were wildly chasing the bouncy red balls down seven flights of stairs, they were each thinking, *I wish I had that blue squeaky toy.* When they *did* have the blue squeaky toy, there were nothing but fights over who got to play with it, and for how long, and whose turn was next.

Nobody could figure out why these dogs, who had been such good friends for over a year, were suddenly so contentious. They should have been the happiest dogs in all the known kingdoms. They had the most luxurious silk pillows to sleep on (as well as every bed—even if there was somebody in it—in any of the 247 bedrooms in both castles combined), the finest and most exotic cuisine (muskrat mixture, chipmunk chews, kangaroo kibble) prepared daily by the royal chefs, so many toys the courtiers were constantly tripping over them and finding them under the many sofa cushions (and still occasionally discovering that their court shoes had been chewed on), and more freedom than was probably good for them. Limits are important and necessary, after all.

The dogs weren't sure why they were so cranky with each other, either. It just seemed there was something in the air that made them feel all prickly and cross.

And then there *was* something in the air. Rain—lots of it.

The rain started the day a rumor reached the

castle at Beaurivage of a woman who had washed ashore about a year before in a village far, far, far downstream, who hadn't been able to remember anything about how she had gotten into the river—or anything at all, really. She apparently had recently regained her memory.

There were no further details, but of course everyone thought of their queen, Olympia, who had fallen into the river the year before.

It kept raining. For days and days and days. Then everybody in Beaurivage—not just the dogs—was in a bad mood.

The suspicions that the woman was Olympia persisted. But no more rumors arrived, and neither did Olympia. Since everyone believed that the first thing she would have done upon recovering her memory that she was a *queen* would have been to get back to Beaurivage as fast as possible, and since that hadn't come about, they began to comfort themselves with the belief that the woman downstream was not Olympia. It was an odd coincidence, they agreed, that another woman had fallen into the river at about the same time, but coincidences happened, especially in villages alongside rivers.

After a week or so of steady rain, the downpours tapered off and finally stopped. But the persistent feelings in Beaurivage were those of gloom, discontent, and unease. It was hard to believe that such a short time before, around the time of the dedication of the Zandelphia-Beaurivage Bridge linking the two kingdoms, many residents, including the royals, believed themselves to be the happiest they had ever been.

# 2

*One Year Earlier*

Mr. Ubaldo Appenzeller, the mayor of Granolah, had very few duties. Ribbon cuttings were few and far between because civic improvements required revenue, which Granolah didn't have; there were no meetings because there was nothing to discuss; and no handshaking was necessary since he already knew everybody in town.

So he went fishing. A lot.

That particular day he'd gone upstream from the village since several other Granolahans were fishing downstream, and he wanted to make sure he got the fish before the fish could get to the other fishers.

He pulled on his waders and slopped through the reeds and weeds into the river. He flung his fishing line out into the water, admiring the silvery pattern it made as it spun through the air and hit the surface. Being able to cast a beautiful line was an excellent quality in a mayor, he thought. He gave his rod a little congratulatory jiggle and frowned when his hook seemed to be stuck on something. He yanked harder and the hook stayed stuck.

He waded a little farther out into the river and saw that his hook was caught on a pile of clothing. Now that was just annoying. The main plank of his election—in fact, the only plank—had been the cleanup of the river. As congenial as most of the Granolahans were in general, when it came to the river they seemed to think it was their town dump. With a lot of nagging and some serious penalties (an afternoon in the stocks, a day spent standing in the corner, a week without doughnuts) he had finally, he thought, gotten them to stop throwing their trash into their pretty stretch of the river. And now there was a mess in there, and who was supposed to do the actual cleaning up? That was just too much to require of one's mayor.

Grumpily, Mr. Appenzeller sloshed out far enough to grab hold of the bundle and pull it in. And it was heavy! Not until he got it close enough to shore for it to drag on the bottom did he realize that the clothes were inhabited. He knew this because whatever was in them began struggling. He was so startled he let out a very unmayoral squeal before hauling the bundle up onto solid ground.

There was so much sodden fabric wound around the floater that Mr. Appenzeller at first couldn't tell what was hidden in the folds. As he stood watching the struggle going on inside the sopping clothing, a dripping wet lump of fur worked its way to the top of the mess and stood with its teeth chattering, uttering pitiful little whimpers. By reflex, Mr. Appenzeller reached out to the poor creature, which responded by baring its fangs and snapping at the outstretched hand. As Mr. Appenzeller retracted his hand in shock, a head popped out of the wet clothing, its eyes wide and frightened. The little animal flung itself on the person's neck, making hysterical sounds.

Arms came out of the soggy heap, frantically pushing the animal away. And the more the arms pushed, the harder the animal tried to wrap itself around the person's neck.

"Stop! Stop! Stop!" the person cried in a voice full of fear and bubbles.

Mr. Appenzeller wasn't the kind of man to ignore a plea for help, but he'd already had a good look at that animal's fangs and he didn't want to get any better acquainted with them. He dithered for a moment, then grabbed his fishing creel and popped it over the hyperactive animal, scooping it inside. He slammed the lid shut and pulled the buckles tight while the creel bounced around in his arms, issuing alarming yowls.

"Oh, thank you," the waterlogged person said. "I don't know what that animal was trying to do, but it scared me to death."

"Do you think you can stand up?" Mr. Appenzeller asked. "I apologize for not helping you," he said, "but as you can see—" He extended the agitated fishing creel.

The pile of wet clothing struggled around at the riverside, grabbing first a reed, which uprooted, and then a boulder, which offered sufficient support for it to become upright. Then Mr. Appenzeller could see that the clothing fell into a gown with a voluminous skirt and an embroidered bodice, and that the river survivor was a female of middle years.

"Of course, of course," the woman said. She stood, leaning against the boulder, trying to adjust her clothing and the stringy strands of her hair.

"Are you all right?" he asked, which seemed a perfectly ludicrous question considering that she had been floating in a river for who-knew-how-long with a wild animal inside her dress.

She looked down at herself, then flexed each arm and swiveled her neck around. "I seem to be. I think everything is working as it should. Where am I?"

"Forgive me," Mr. Appenzeller said, juggling the fishing creel. "My name is Ubaldo Appenzeller. I'm mayor of the village of Granolah, which is where you are. Where did you—ah—enter the river?"

It was a bit of a ticklish question, as he didn't know if she'd fallen in by accident, been pitched in by an angry mob, or flung herself into the river in despair over some tragic situation.

"Well, I suppose it must have been—" She scratched her wet head. "How odd. I haven't the slightest idea. I can't remember at all how it happened."

"Perfectly understandable," Mr. Appenzeller said. "You've been through quite an ordeal. Perhaps if you tell me your name, I'll be able to make a connection with one of our nearby towns. Well, the kingdom we're part of is so far from everything that we're not actually nearby to anything, but I'll do my best."

"Certainly." The woman was now sitting on the boulder. "My name is—" Again she paused. "Huh. I *must* know my own name, but I can't seem to . . ." She trailed off. After a moment, she lifted the hem of her skirt and looked down at her feet. "I have only one shoe," she said, "but it's a very nice one, isn't it?"

The mayor looked. The shoe was silvery, with a bow on the toe. It was rather the worse for wear at the moment, but he could see that it had once been, indeed, a very nice shoe. He knew this because his wife, Wivinia, loved shoes. Her shoe collection was so large that it required its own cupboard in their cozy cottage, and she was primarily responsible for keeping Granolah's shoemaker in business.

"And this dress," she went on. "It's brocade, isn't it? Or damask, or something like that? It seems I was all gussied up for something when I went in the river. But for the life of me, I can't remember what it was." She shivered.

Mr. Appenzeller sighed. Clearly, his quiet morning of fishing was over. "Come on, then," he said. "Let's get you where you can dry off and warm up and then we'll see what comes back to you. Some rest and a hot meal can do wonders."

She limped off along the path to town accompanied by Mr. Appenzeller, a fat little man juggling an unruly fishing creel.

———

WARM DRY CLOTHES, a hot meal, and a nap did nothing to refresh the woman's memory, though they did refresh her looks—and quite a handsome, well-set-up matron she was.

It had begun to cross Mr. Appenzeller's mind that he and Wivinia might be having a long-term house-guest—which is exactly what they ended up with. After some days with the Appenzellers, the stranger suggested they find a name for her since she wasn't remembering anything, and none of their unmethodical inquiries had turned up any information about her. "You can't keep calling me 'her,'" she said.

"Do you have any suggestions?" Wivinia Appenzeller asked. "Any name that strikes your fancy? Any name you especially love?"

The stranger pondered for a moment. "Hmm. Camilla? Diana? Olympia? Bathsheba? Cinderella? Guinevere? Fatima? None of those seem quite right. Oh. I know. Angelica! Isn't that a pretty name? Angelica. It's so . . . so angelic. Does that seem presumptuous? I mean, I'm not suggesting I'm angelic."

"Of course not," Wivinia said. "But it is a lovely name. And it suits you."

INDEED IT DID. Angelica was always eager to help in any way around the house, though she was surprisingly

11

inept at even the simplest chores. At first she burned anything she tried to cook, pulled the flowers out of the garden and left the weeds, and didn't even know where to begin when it came to laundry. She must have lost her memories of how to perform these basic survival tasks along with all her other memories.

She was a quick and eager learner, though, and soon could prepare a simple meal, sweep out the cottage, and haul water from the well without spilling any. She and Mrs. Appenzeller sewed a wardrobe for her that was a little out of the ordinary since the visitor always wanted extra embellishments on her garments—more ruffles, bows (especially bows), and trimmings were always better than fewer. Bonding the two women was their love of shoes, which the visitor was able to buy from the village shoemaker with a supply of gold coins found sewn into the hem of the dress she'd washed up in. No one could figure out why anyone would have a hemful of money, but there it was.

Before long, everyone in Granolah was calling the new arrival Angie, and had accepted her presence as part of their village life. The only problem was with the animal that had been trapped inside her dress. He was miserable, as well as terribly noisy, inside the fishing creel. But when the Appenzellers tried to dump him outside in the woods, he raced them back to their cottage and sped straight for their visitor, who was terrified of him.

"Perhaps he was your pet in the life you've forgotten," Ubaldo finally suggested. "Maybe he remembers what you don't." He handed Angelica a scrap of platypus left over from their previous night's dinner. "Here. Try feeding him. See how he reacts to you."

"*You* try," she said. "I'm afraid he'll bite my hand off."

"It's you he seems so fond of," Ubaldo said nervously, pressing the platypus scrap into her palm. He flipped up the lid of the creel. "Don't cringe," he encouraged her. "Be brave."

The animal jumped out of the creel, looked around, and headed for Angie, fast as lightning. He scaled her like a mountaineer, bypassing the platypus and nestling on her shoulder with his nose in her ear, making pitiful little mewling noises.

"See?" Mr. Appenzeller said. "He likes you. Better than platypus even."

Angie sat as still as a post, her eyes wide and terrified, the platypus forgotten in her hand. But when all the animal did was continue his whimpering in her ear, she gradually relaxed. Tentatively, she patted his furry back, which caused him to snuggle even closer.

"Maybe you're right," she whispered. "Maybe he *was* my pet."

"Sure looks that way to me," Ubaldo said. He removed one of the leather straps from the fishing creel, and said, "We can put a collar on him, and a rope. That way we can keep control of him." He dangled the strap toward the woman. "He'd probably like it better if you did it."

It took some coaxing and jockeying by both of them, but finally they got the collar on the creature's neck. The length of rope tied to it seemed unnecessary considering how closely he huddled against the woman's skirt.

"I guess he needs a name now," Ubaldo said. "Anything come into your mind?"

Angie looked down at him. "No. So why don't we call him—I don't know—Fenleigh, let's say."

"Pretty highfalutin name for a—whatever he is— but I guess that's his name now."


TO EVERYONE'S SURPRISE, Angie made a friend of the village's most troubled resident—Lazy Susan.

Lazy Susan was Sleeping Beauty's half sister, and she had never gotten over her resentment that Beauty was so much younger, so much more spoiled, and had grown up in a castle. Lazy Susan had been left behind in Granolah with her grandparents when her mother, a pretty young widow, married the monarch of a distant kingdom and went off to forget she'd had any life before that. By doing absolutely *nothing*, Beauty had won herself a handsome prince, while Susan herself did a *few* things (though none of them very well, or very fast) and couldn't even get the local sheepshearer to give her a second look. And now that she was past her prime, the sheep wouldn't look at her, either.

Most of the Granolahans were pretty tired of hearing about all this, especially since Lazy Susan wouldn't take any advice, such as "Get over it," or "Stop frowning so much," or "Learn to do something really well." But Angie, always accompanied by a meek Fenleigh now, was willing to listen endlessly to Lazy Susan complain, or mourn, or rehash the past. This caused some Granolahans to believe she really was angelic.

In these ways, a year went by, smoothly and peacefully, as almost every year in Granolah went. And during that time, almost everybody forgot that Angie hadn't always been there.

# 3

Then, early one morning, Wivinia and Ubaldo Appenzeller were wakened from a sound sleep by a shriek coming from Angie's room. They scrambled out of bed, tripping over their nightshirts, their nightcaps askew, Ubaldo wielding a pitchfork that he'd kept under his bed for years in the event of an emergency that had never happened. Until now.

When they burst through the door of Angie's room, they found her sitting up in bed screaming her head off, with Fenleigh buried under a pillow, only his rear end and tail sticking out.

"What is it?" Ubaldo stood in the doorway, his pitchfork raised.

Wivinia rushed to Angie, but when she tried to put her arms around her, Angie shoved her away and screamed louder.

After a moment, Ubaldo and Wivinia could tell that Angie was screaming words. And the words were, "Where am I? Who are you?" and something that sounded like, "Get me Rollo!"

Trying to reassure her required more screaming by Ubaldo and Wivinia. This went on for a while, with nobody listening to anyone else, until all three of them were hoarse and coughing, and finally had to stop yelling.

"Who's Rollo?" Ubaldo croaked, as Angie was rasping, "Who are you?"

"Why, Angie, what do you mean?" Wivinia asked. "We're the Appenzellers. Ubaldo and Wivinia. You've lived with us for a year."

"I have done no such thing," Angie said. "And why are you calling me Angie?" She grabbed Fenleigh by the tail and yanked him out from under the pillow. "Get out of there."

"Oh," Wivinia said. "I don't think Fenleigh likes being treated that way."

"Who cares about that?" Angie said. "And how do you know his name, but not mine?"

Wivinia scratched her head. "You picked his name.

And yours, too. Don't you remember?" Turning to Ubaldo, she said, "I think she's lost her memory again."

"Lost my memory?" Angie said. "What do you mean *again*?"

So the Appenzellers told her the story of how she had come to Granolah, and what the last year had been like for her.

"I did laundry?" Angie asked, appalled. "I swept and carried *water*?"

"Well, yes," Ubaldo said. "The same as the rest of us. Why shouldn't you?"

She drew herself up in the bed and slung Fenleigh around her shoulders like a stole. "Because I am Queen Olympia of the kingdom of Beaurivage. And today is my daughter's wedding day."

Well, Ubaldo almost fell on the floor laughing. When he recovered, he said, "For goodness' sake, Angie, you had us scared to death. I have to say, this is about the best practical joke I ever heard. Queen Olympia, indeed!" And he started laughing all over again.

Wivinia, however, didn't find it so funny. She patted her chest over her heart and said, "Don't ever do that again, Angie, please. You gave me palpitations.

You know we wish you could recover your memory, but this is just cruel—and so unlike you."

"Hah!" Olympia said, getting out of bed. "I *have* recovered my memory. And I *am* Queen Olympia. It's all coming back to me. I fell off the terrace of Beaurivage Castle into the river during Marigold's wedding. And you're telling me that was a year ago? I must get back to Beaurivage immediately. No telling what's gone wrong in my absence. Get me a carriage! And something better to wear than this"—with two fingers she held out the nightgown she and Wivinia had lovingly made together—"this rubbish."

Wivinia had never seen a real queen, of course, but she'd heard plenty about their behavior from Lazy Susan. And she suspected she was witnessing some of that behavior just then. It was certainly unattractive—and nothing like the way Angie would have behaved. Wivinia said so to Ubaldo.

"You think so? Really?"

"I do. That would explain a lot about the fancy clothes and the gold coins in the dress and the way she arrived here. I think she really is a queen."

Being mayor suddenly seemed a very puny thing to Mr. Appenzeller. And thinking that a queen had spent a year sleeping in the tiny room that had once been the potato and turnip storage space made him feel a bit light-headed.

"A carriage! Now!" Olympia commanded. "Where are my clothes?"

Obediently Wivinia lifted the lid on a chest in the corner, and pulled out the single silver shoe and the white-and-gold dress Olympia had been wearing when they'd first seen her. "We did our best," she said, "but we couldn't get all the stains out." She gestured to several garments hanging from a peg on the wall. "Those are what you've been wearing."

Olympia gave her a horrified look. "You can't be serious."

Wivinia shrugged and nodded.

"Very well," Olympia said in resignation. "I'll just have to wear my old dress. Where's that other shoe?"

"In the river, I suppose," Wivinia said. To tell the truth, she was feeling pretty offended by this high-handedness from someone she'd sheltered for a whole year. She could see that her friend Angie was truly gone, and she didn't care at all for the new person who'd arrived in her place, queen or not. Wivinia was sure that if *she'd* been a queen, she'd have been a lot nicer to her subjects. This Queen Olympia was an example of why peasants staged revolts.

"Well, what am I supposed to wear home?"

Wivinia opened the chest again, displaying the collection of shoes from Granolah's shoemaker. None of them were as fancy as the silver one. There was no need for such shoes in Granolah, but they were certainly well made and plenty stylish enough for village life.

"I'm glad to see I didn't forget *all* my preferences," Olympia said, inspecting the shoes. "I'll take . . . these." She pulled out a pair of red sphinx-leather pumps with high stacked heels. She turned to Ubaldo. "You! What are you waiting for? I need that carriage!"

"Uh, we don't have any carriages in Granolah. We never go anywhere."

"Then you figure out a way to get me back to Beaurivage while I get dressed. And remember, I can sentence you to death. Or worse."

*Or worse?* Ubaldo thought. *What was worse?* Since he didn't really want to know, he turned around and went out the door, still in his nightshirt, to find some help getting this harridan out of Granolah forever.

It took him a while, since he had to explain what was going on to the first few people he encountered, including the worse-than-death threats. After that, they spread the word around the village as fast as they could. It was even juicier news than Angie's arrival. And he had to wake up Lazy Susan, to see if Angie's best friend could get her to calm down and quit making unreasonable demands and threats. Truthfully, he just wanted somebody else to deal with her since he was having such little success at it.

By the time Olympia was dressed, which fortunately took a long time, considering all the repairs she needed to make after a year of cosmetic neglect, the mayor had rounded up a couple of mules, a wheelbarrow, and Lazy Susan, also still in her nightie.

The look on Olympia's face when she came out of the cottage and saw what Ubaldo had concocted for her was something Wivinia would call to mind for years afterward whenever she needed a good laugh.

"Hi, Angie," Lazy Susan said. "What's going on? I haven't been up this early in . . . well, never."

"Who are you?" Olympia asked imperiously.

Lazy Susan gave Ubaldo a look that indicated she hadn't believed him at first, but now she did. "I'm— I'm Lazy Susan. I've been your best friend for the whole last year."

"I find that very hard to believe," Olympia said. Lazy Susan looked as if she were about to cry. Then, turning to Ubaldo, Olympia said, "You expect me to arrive in Beaurivage in this *contraption*? Pulled by *mules*?"

"It's . . . it's the best we have to offer," the mayor

stammered. "Some of our Granolahans made great sacrifices to give you these things—*their* things. And they aren't too happy about it. They really should be compensated." He trailed off, sure he was wasting his breath.

To his surprise, Angie—or Olympia, or whoever she was—said, "Are you suggesting I'm a thief? I pay for whatever I take." She bent, felt the hem of her dress, and straightened, her eyes flashing fire. "Where are my gold coins? My dressmaker uses them to weight my hems so my skirts hang correctly, but I can also use them for purchases."

"You've already spent them," Ubaldo said. "In the year you've been here. Mostly on shoes."

This seemed to make sense to her. "Very well. Then I'll have to compensate you once I get back to Beaurivage. And I'll also return these"—she pointed to the wheelbarrow and the mules—"*things*. I certainly will have no further use for them. Now let's get started." She stepped into the wheelbarrow, rolling her eyes as she did so. Fenleigh clung to her shoulder. "Well? Who's going to drive this thing for me?" In the silence that followed, she pointed to Lazy Susan. "You!"

"But I can't," she began, and then paused. "So you want me to come with you? You did say we'd be friends forever."

"*I* said a thing like that?" Olympia asked, incredulous.

Lazy Susan nodded.

"Hmmm," Olympia mused. "Well, all the better. You can be my maid as well as the driver. But you'll have to ride one of those." She pointed to the mule. "This"—she patted the side of the wheelbarrow—"is all mine. And Fenleigh's, too, of course."

"I need to get dressed," Lazy Susan said. "And I know I can get you to Beaurivage. I was there once before with Beauty." She sneered at the name. "For the triplets' weddings."

"You were at that wedding?" Olympia asked. "Wasn't it lovely? My daughters may not be the smartest girls, but they did marry well. Didn't I look splendid in that peach mousseline?"

"I have no idea. I was so far back in the crowd I couldn't see a thing," Lazy Susan said, hurrying away to dress and pack.

Olympia drummed her fingers on the side of the wheelbarrow until Lazy Susan returned with a gunnysack full of her clothes, which she tied onto one mule. Then she mounted the other one.

"Good-bye, everyone," Lazy Susan said, waving. "I'm going to the castle at Beaurivage with Queen

Olympia. You can tell that to Beauty if you see her. Ciao!"

Once the wheelbarrow procession reached the edge of town, which took only a few minutes, Ubaldo turned to Wivinia and said, "I hope we never see that woman again. I wouldn't ever be able to trust her to stay whoever she said she was. Do you think everybody will blame me for rescuing her from the river? Do you think that will hurt my chances for reelection?"

"It might, dear," Wivinia said. "But they also liked her for a long time, and they know you couldn't have had any idea how it would work out. So you'll want to keep reminding them that you're the one who figured out how to get rid of someone who, with her memory regained, would have been very unpleasant to have in Granolah. Make it seem like your idea."

"Thank you, Wivinia. I'll use that in my campaign slogan. I just hope she remembers to pay for the mules."

They watched the puff of dust that was Olympia, Lazy Susan, and the mules recede into the distance.

# 4

A few days before Olympia finally showed up, Christian, King of Zandelphia, and Marigold, formerly Princess of Beaurivage and now Queen of Zandelphia, had their first fight ever. They were sitting on the new terrace outside the crystal cave-castle at Zandelphia, enjoying their breakfast, the sunshine after all that rain, and the *Daily Discourse*. Usually Christian didn't mind Marigold reading over his shoulder and sharing her opinions on the day's news. For the whole last year, their first as a married couple, he'd loved hearing whatever was on her mind. But this morning, for reasons he only recognized later, as she leaned on his shoulder and crunched her toast in his ear, he had to restrain himself from shrugging her off. Then she said, "Look at that. Alison Wonderland has gotten lost again. That girl just never learns."

"Marigold, my blossom," Christian said through gritted teeth, "could you please stop leaning on me and chomping in my ear? Please." He added the extra "please" in an effort to sound not as irritated as he really was.

But Marigold, after years of friendship and a year of marriage, knew him too well. She knew all his tones of voice, though he had never used this particular one with her. She jerked upright, and swallowed her toast so fast she was afraid it would get stuck in her throat and prevent her from delivering the piece of her mind she thought Christian was entitled to. Fortunately it went right down, allowing her to say, "I hope you will never speak to me in that tone again, for as long as you live."

Chris pretended innocence and said, "What tone is that, precious?" Of course he knew what tone, but as so often happens, people are reluctant to own up to their own transgressions, even though they know such avoidance doesn't usually get them anywhere except in more hot water.

Marigold gave Christian a glare that he had never seen before, and said, "You know exactly what I mean.

Don't make it worse by denying it." Now she was standing, facing him with her hands on her hips.

For some reason (guilt, probably—such a troublesome emotion), this made him mad all over again. How dare she look at him like that after everything he had done for her? Including saving her from an arranged marriage, or certain death at the hands of her mother, Queen Olympia—who, thankfully, had fallen into the river before either threat could be completed. He said, "Perhaps you should pay some attention to your own tone of voice."

Marigold blinked. "What? What did you say?"

"I think you heard me," he said, making it worse.

She narrowed her eyes. "You do remember that I know witches and fairies and imps, all of whom could do you some harm if I asked them to."

"Are you threatening me?"

"Can you think of a reason why I shouldn't?"

His pride prevented him from saying, "Because you love me too much to do such a thing." It also prevented him from saying, "I'm sorry. I overreacted. I shouldn't have spoken to you the way I did." Instead, he unwisely said, "Do what you think you have to do."

She looked at him as if she didn't even know him, then turned and left the terrace, with Flopsy, Mopsy, and Topsy at her heels. He watched her go with a chill around his heart. She *did* know witches and fairies and imps. But would she really use them against him? Didn't she love him enough not to do that? Didn't she love him at all? And how, in ten quick minutes, had they gone from a peaceful breakfast on the terrace to death threats? It was as if some toxic breeze had blown over them and poisoned the air they breathed, turning them into alternate versions of themselves, versions that were stupid and unpleasant and mean. They were acting like—like *Olympia*.

# 5

On the long trip back to Beaurivage by mule and wheelbarrow, Olympia complained nonstop. She was tired, she was sore, she was sunburned, she was dirty, she was bored—and whatever was wrong, she wanted Lazy Susan to do something about it. Lazy Susan also was tired, sore (*she* was the one riding the mule, after all), etc., and after the first day she was ready to muzzle Olympia and was wondering why in the world she'd ever wanted to come with her. The queen was *nothing* like her dear friend Angie, who was so kind and modest and appreciative.

The only thing that cheered Lazy Susan up was knowing that at the end of the journey there would be a castle with clean sheets and hot water and good food. She could take a bubble bath to get the smell of mule off her, eat a hearty meal, and sleep for a week. Maybe two.

"Fenleigh and I are hungry," Olympia announced. "Get us something to eat."

"You already ate the last of the food we brought from Granolah," Lazy Susan said. "We have nothing left."

"Then *find* something," Olympia commanded. "We're *hungry!*"

Lazy Susan stopped the mules at the edge of a stream. Finding food and drink for them was easy enough, and required no work from her—just the way she liked it.

At the end of a path leading away from the stream was a tiny cottage with a profusion of wild roses growing up the side and across the roof. Lazy Susan balked at the idea of walking all the way up that path. And then all the way back *carrying* something. But with one glance at Olympia, her face a storm cloud, her arms crossed over her substantial chest, Lazy Susan sighed, dismounted, and began trudging, aggrieved, up the path.

She opened the garden gate, knocked at the cottage door, and waited. No one came. She knocked again, and looked back down the path at Olympia, who remained stone-faced and hungry. When still no one came, Lazy Susan decided to walk around the cottage. Perhaps there were some fruit trees or a vegetable garden.

As she rounded the corner of the building, she was stopped in her tracks at the sight of a rotund gentleman with a full head of white hair, wearing britches and a long-underwear shirt, sweating profusely as he tried to uproot a stump. A string of incomprehensible syllables issued from his mouth and, though Lazy Susan couldn't understand them, there was no mistaking their intent. Cautiously, she cleared her throat.

Startled, the man looked up from the stump and flushed a bright red. He said some more words, none of which she could understand but that seemed apologetic in tone. She shrugged and asked slowly, "Do . . . you . . . speak . . . English?"

"Oh, yes, of course," he said. "Did you overhear me while I was wrestling with that stump?"

"I did," she said. "I couldn't understand anything you said, but I definitely got the idea you weren't happy."

"I was indeed cursing," he admitted, "and I apologize. I find it satisfying to curse in languages other than my native one, but so many travelers from different parts come along this road, I'm never sure when one who understands the language I'm using will happen by and be offended."

"I speak only one language," Lazy Susan said, "and I'm not exactly an expert at that one. So I wasn't offended in the least."

"Is there something I can help you with?" the gentleman asked.

"Oh. Yes. My—" She stopped. She couldn't really call Olympia her friend now that she was no longer Angie, which caused a brief painful pinch to Lazy Susan's heart. "My traveling companion and I have come a long way, and we've got a long way to go yet, and we've run out of food. We were wondering if maybe—"

Before she could go any further, he said, "Most assuredly. It would be my pleasure, and a great treat for me. I rarely have anyone to dine with since I live so far from the nearest village. And while many travelers pass by, few stop for a meal. You're both much more than welcome."

He strode around to the front of the cottage with Lazy Susan trailing him. When he spotted Olympia in the wheelbarrow at the end of the path, he waved to her and then beckoned for her to join them. She didn't move. He beckoned again.

"I'll go get her." Lazy Susan sighed. By the time they'd eaten, that would make two round trips on that same path, which was more walking than she normally did in several days.

"Where's the food?" Olympia asked as Lazy Susan approached the wheelbarrow.

"He wants us to come inside. He'll feed us in there."

"Are you crazy? We don't know anything about him. These parts are full of fairy folk and sorcerers and gremlins. If he's one, and knows who I am, who can tell what he'll do."

Lazy Susan had had enough. "I'm sufficiently hungry to take a chance. You decide for yourself."

The front door was wide open as Lazy Susan came back along the path, and the white-haired man waited on the threshold, his arms spread expansively.

"*Bok, daw-daw,* and *nark!*" he exclaimed.

Lazy Susan stopped. Maybe Olympia was right—apparently these parts *were* inhabited by some very strange sorts. "I'm sorry?" she said.

"I'm welcoming you," he said. "*Bok* is Croatian for hello, *daw-daw* is Jutlandish for hello, and *nark* is Phorhépechan for hello."

"Oh."

"I could have said *aloha* but that also means good-bye. As does *ayubowan*—that's Sri Lankan—and I don't want to be telling you good-bye so soon. Not at all."

"I see. And how is it you know all these words?" She stood unmoving on the path.

"I've lived alone here for a long time. Tending my garden and making little knickknacks in my workshop has passed some of the time, but learning languages, for which I seem to have a great facility, has filled the rest of it. It's been mentally stimulating, as well as allowing me to converse with any odd stranger who passes by on the road. And some of them, I assure you, have been very odd."

Lazy Susan exhaled the breath she'd been holding, and started walking again.

"Forgive me for not introducing myself," he said as she reached the door. "My name is Stan Lucasa. And you are . . . ?"

"I'm Lazy Susan. Sleeping Beauty is my half sister. Do you know her? She married a prince who fell in love with her while she was asleep. Doesn't that strike you as peculiar?"

"I'm sorry. I can't say that I know her or her prince. And love is a mysterious thing—something I appreciate and never question. Well, welcome, Susan." She noticed that he didn't use her adjective. He pointed to the wheelbarrow where Olympia still sat. "Your companion isn't coming?"

"I don't know," Lazy Susan said. "But we don't have to wait for her."

The inside of the cottage was a complete surprise. Lazy Susan had been expecting a bachelor environment—sparse furnishings, piles of dirty laundry, and inches of dust. Not only was the place immaculate, it was tastefully filled with lively objects that were decorative as well as functional. The walls were lined with shelves of carved birds and animals in fanciful shapes.

The round table was covered with an embroidered cloth; platters overflowed with delicious-looking concoctions. She stopped, her mouth open. "How in the world—"

Mr. Lucasa pulled out a chair with an elaborately carved back and a seat cushion made from a cheerful striped fabric. "I like to cook," he said. "Have a seat."

She sat, still speechless. Mr. Lucasa apparently liked to cook *fast*. She'd seen enough magic in her time to be glad that if his methods were magical, they produced delicious-looking food instead of noxious smoke or lightning bolts.

He handed her a heaping plate, then filled a plate for himself and sat across from her. He ate quickly and tidily, and was on his second plateful while she was still savoring her first.

Suddenly the front door was flung open so hard it hit the wall and bounced back. Olympia pushed it open again, and stood on the threshold in her stained and rumpled gown, Fenleigh draped over the shoulders. "You left me," she said, glaring.

Lazy Susan shrugged, her mouth full of delectable roasted meat. "You didn't want to come," she managed.

"Were you intending to bring me something? Or were you going to eat it all yourself?"

Mr. Lucasa had come to his feet, a large napkin in his hand, when the door banged open, but Olympia ignored him.

"This is Mr. Lucasa," Lazy Susan said, gesturing to him with her fork. "He made this feast. It's good."

"Madam," Mr. Lucasa said, "please join us." He waved his hand over the table, on which there remained plenty to eat.

Olympia's eyes glittered hungrily. "Very well." She made her way regally to the table, where she, and Fenleigh, too, ate like lumberjacks.

This pleased Mr. Lucasa immensely. "That is a special dish I invented," he said. "Squab with *flab* and *moron*."

Lazy Susan dropped her fork and coughed. "Flabs and morons?"

Mr. Lucasa laughed a hearty laugh. "*Flab* is Gaelic

for mushroom, and *moron* is Welsh for carrot. Perfectly harmless, I guarantee it."

"And very good, too," Olympia said, her mouth full. "Quite excellent. Would you like a job at Beaurivage Castle? We can always use another chef in the kitchens."

"We don't know anything about him, remember?" Lazy Susan reminded her primly.

"I know enough." Olympia waved her hand dismissively. "He can cook. That's all I need to know."

"I do like to cook," he agreed. "You said Beaurivage Castle?"

"Where else did you think Queen Olympia would live?"

"You're a queen?" he asked. When she nodded, still chewing, he cast a glance out the window to where the mules stood, eating the flowers by his front gate, the wheelbarrow on its side.

Olympia saw the look, and drew herself up so haughtily that she could have been wearing a crown instead of a tattered and dirty dress. "I may not appear very royal right now, but I've just been through an extraordinary experience. I assure you that once I get you back to Beaurivage Castle you will see how regal I can be."

He laughed and gestured around himself. "I live *here*. I'm not looking for a job."

"Trifles." Olympia sniffed. "I'll send some of my minions to tend to things while you're away."

"Your minions?" he said.

"You know. Lackeys. Flunkies. Underlings."

"I know what they are," he said.

Lazy Susan could see him thinking, looking around his pretty cottage as if imprinting it on his mind, making a picture he could take with him. She'd done the same thing (only much faster) when she left her familiar surroundings in Granolah.

"You can do that?" he asked. "Send someone to take care of things while I'm gone?"

"With the wave of one hand," Olympia said, demonstrating by waving the wishbone from the squab. Then she pulled the wishbone apart with both hands and crowed, "I win! I get my wish!"

Both Lazy Susan and Mr. Lucasa refrained from reminding her that you always win when you're the only one playing.

"I haven't been away from here in a very long time," he mused. "It might do me good. I can always come back." He trailed off into muttering in some other language.

Suddenly he sat up straight and said, "All right. I'll do it."

Olympia pushed her empty plate away and rose, picking her teeth delicately with her pinkie. "Let's get started," she said.

"Not so fast. I need to get ready," Mr. Lucasa told her.

Olympia sat again and took a spoon to the dish of marshmallow mousse. "Well, hurry up."

Mr. Lucasa didn't. He took his time packing up the leftover food and washing the dishes. Then he got together some clothes and other necessities in a leather satchel. By the time he was ready, Olympia had finished the marshmallow mousse and was tapping her foot.

"You can ride on the other mule, I guess," Lazy Susan said, leading the way back to their transportation.

Mr. Lucasa tied his bundles onto the mule carrying Lazy Susan's things, and said, "I believe I'll walk." He patted his round belly. "It'll be good for me. At least until I start to *tenjack*. That's 'to limp' in Malaysian."

FOR SEVERAL DAYS they traveled, living on the excellent provisions Mr. Lucasa had brought from his kitchen. Then, plodding along an unusually wide lane through rolling countryside, Olympia ordered, "Stop!"

Lazy Susan pulled the mules to a halt and looked back to see Olympia standing up in the wobbly wheelbarrow, looking around her. "I know this place," she said. "I've been here before."

"I have, too," Lazy Susan said. "Beaurivage is near."

"I was here once on a picnic during a fox hunt," Olympia said. "We're getting close to the castle."

"Fox hunt?" Mr. Lucasa repeated. "You mean . . . to *kill* them?"

"It's a *sport*," Olympia said. "Nobody cares about the foxes. It's all for fun."

"Not much fun for the foxes," Mr. Lucasa said, giving Olympia a hard stare. "I'll bet the foxes don't like that sport at all."

"Who cares what the foxes think? I do love a sport that requires a costume. You should see my favorite Riding to the Hounds outfit. Bronze taffeta with bright blue buttons and lapels. So stylish. And the hat has a little foxtail on it."

Mr. Lucasa continued to give her that look. "Some fox probably needed that tail."

"Not anymore he doesn't," Olympia said. "Keep going. We're almost there. And I have a lot of unfinished business to take care of."

# 6

Edric had been trying to get up the courage to ask Wendolyn's father for her hand for several months. He'd loved her for years and, though they were both trolls, who lived a very long time, he was tired of waiting to declare himself. But whenever he thought the time was right, something would happen. A storm would prevent him from paying the visit, or he'd get a toothache, or a cold—but the truth was he was just plain chicken. He thought her father would say yes. After all, Ed's Tooth Troll business, which had replaced the Tooth Fairy's inept operation, was doing very well, and he was on best-friend terms with King

Swithbert of Beaurivage, in whose castle he lived. Wendolyn's father would surely find Ed an excellent prospect for a son-in-law.

Ed just wasn't sure he was such an excellent prospect as a husband. He was old (which wasn't unusual for trolls), he was ugly (though not any uglier than most trolls), and he was horribly shy when it came to girls (though not shy at all with anybody else).

He'd watched how Christian and Marigold were together—so splendid to look at, so loving and kind and playful with each other, so helpful and respectful, and such good rulers of Zandelphia across the river. But he couldn't imagine being such a perfect spouse day after day. He made too many mistakes, lost his temper too often, and cheated at cards (but so did Swithbert, who was the only person Ed played with, so it usually worked out okay).

One morning he woke up and thought, *Today's the day. Nobody's perfect. I love Wendolyn. I'll let her decide if she wants to get married to me. If I don't ask, how can she tell?*

He whistled while he dressed and went down to breakfast, ignoring Bub and Cate growling at each other in one of the side passages of the castle. He stopped to pick up a blue squeaky toy lying on the stairs and put it in his pocket. Somebody might trip over that and fall down the steps.

"Morning, Ed," King Swithbert said from the head of the long table where he was giving an egg in an eggcup a good whack. His ruddy cheeks and bright eyes belied his advanced age. In fact, in the year that Olympia had been gone, he seemed to have become younger. "Blast! A runny egg again! When will that cook learn to get it right?"

"You could send it back," Ed said. "You *are* the king."

"Oh, I know," Swithbert said. "But I don't want to make him feel bad." He sighed and took a bite of the runny egg, making a face.

"The pigeons are flying again after all that rain, so I'm sending a p-mail to Wendolyn's father today," Ed said, "asking for her hand. And the rest of her, too."

"High time," Swithbert said. "I'm not the best person to be giving marital advice, considering what a disaster my marriage to Olympia was, but I hope it works out for you. What else would I wish for my best friend, and the most enthusiastic card partner I've ever had?"

"Just take a look at Marigold and Christian if you want to feel encouraged about marriage," Ed said. "So it seems to be six of one half, a dozen of another."

"Whatever you say, Ed. Good luck. And yes, Chris and my daughter do seem to have figured out how to do it right."

At that moment Christian came into the dining room panting as if he had run all the way from Zandelphia to Beaurivage. "I don't know what to do," he gasped. "Marigold is threatening to kill me."

MEANWHILE, Marigold sat in the golden-crystal library room in her cave-castle, crying her eyes out. How could she and Chris have said those things to each other? How could she have threatened him like that? And worse, how could she have *meant* it? He was her sweetheart, her best friend, her bulwark against life's tribulations. And for a few minutes at breakfast, she'd really wanted nothing more than to have him hit with a curse so big and so black that it would take years for him to recover. Did decent people really feel like that about their loved ones, or was there something horribly wrong with her, the way Queen Olympia had always said there was? Had all those years of criticism left her with some scarred and rotten place on her soul?

She erupted into a fresh flood of sobbing that brought Flopsy, Mopsy, and Topsy clustering around her, putting their paws up on her knees, and finally baying along with her.

OLYMPIA'S ENTOURAGE came out of the trees at the edge of the forest. Before them was a long undulant meadow dotted with wildflowers and grazing sheep, all so artfully distributed that it seemed some giant hand had arranged it just for the queen's arrival. In the distance were the hazy towers of Beaurivage Castle, colorful flags flying from the battlements.

"Oh!" Olympia said. "Home! You are shortly going to see some very surprised faces." She rubbed her hands together. "I can't wait."

Lazy Susan gave her mule a little kick in the ribs to get him moving again, but Olympia commanded, "Wait! I can't arrive this way. Lucasa, don't you have something to wear besides that long-underwear top? And Lazy Susan, wash your face and do something about your hair. It's a disgrace." She felt her own hair and looked down at her stained dress. "How can I show up looking like this? It just won't do. You two! Think of something!"

"Why us?" Lazy Susan asked. But Mr. Lucasa was already gathering wildflowers by the bushel. Quickly, he concocted a sort of netting woven from the flowers that he draped over Olympia's skirt, and another that he arranged into her hair. Then he did the same for Lazy Susan while Olympia fussed and primped with her new outfit, gazing at her reflection in a roadside puddle, a remnant of the recent rains.

"Genius!" she said to Mr. Lucasa. "I will make you my new chef *and* my new dressmaker. I believe I'll be setting a style for every woman in Beaurivage. I look so fresh and vernal and youthful, don't you think?"

"Flowers always look good," he said noncommittally.

"Make some wreaths for these mules," she ordered. "Then I can ride one of them into the castle, and you and Lazy Susan can come along with the other one, pulling the wheelbarrow with the bundles. We want to make this look as dignified as we can, under the very unfortunate circumstances. The wheelbarrow was somewhat more comfortable for a long trip, but I think a flower-covered steed makes for a better entrance. Oh, and make a wreath for Fenleigh, too."

Lazy Susan and Mr. Lucasa made the wreaths while Olympia continued to admire herself in the puddle. When the mules were adorned, she hefted herself onto one of them and started off, leaving Lazy Susan and Mr. Lucasa to organize everything else.

Because it was Market Day at the castle, farmers

and peasants from all around the countryside were pouring over the drawbridge and under the portcullis. Olympia had no trouble traveling in with them, obscured by the throng, though she was somewhat annoyed that no one recognized her, or appreciated how fresh, vernal, and youthful she looked.

Mr. Lucasa and Lazy Susan followed her through the crowded bailey where stalls were set up for the sale of homemade craft items (most of which were so ugly and poorly made it was hard to imagine who would want them), baked goods (that were either too sticky, too raw, or too misshapen to be appealing), and local produce (which would probably be all right to eat once the cow patties were washed off).

Suddenly the word "Olympia?" rang out. Olympia turned a wide smile in the direction of the voice, searching the crowd. Her eyes traveled up to a balcony overlooking the bailey—and there stood King Swithbert, his eyes almost popping out of his face. He squeezed them shut, shook his head, and opened them again.

"Olympia?" he asked again, in disbelief and dread.

"Yes, it's me," she called to him. "Surprise! I'll be right up."

Looking around at the crowd of amazed faces now turned toward her, she waved from the back of her mule. "Yes, my loyal subjects," she called gaily. "It is your queen, returned at last."

"It can't be!" she heard. And "I don't believe it." And "What is that she's wearing?" And "I thought she was gone for good." All of which Olympia interpreted in the most complimentary way.

# 7

What about us?" Lazy Susan called after her as Olympia headed for the postern that led directly to Swithbert's quarters.

"Oh, yes. You two take the beasts to the stables." Olympia pointed. "Tell somebody there to return them to Granolah. And make sure they take that horrible wheelbarrow, too. Whoever delivers them can go back to Lucasa's home and tend it until he gets back there. Oh—and tell them to send along a bag of gold pieces. I said I'd compensate the owners of the stuff, and a queen keeps her word. Pathetic as those animals and that conveyance are, they got me home."

(It would turn out that Mr. Appenzeller ignored his wife's advice for the choice of a campaign slogan and instead used Olympia's generous compensation as the inspiration for the slogan in his next mayoral campaign: ELECT APPENZELLER. HE CAN TURN YOUR ASSES INTO GOLD. He lost the election.)

"Then," Olympia went on, "go see Mrs. Clover, the head housekeeper. Tell her I sent you, and why." She turned her back on them and vanished.

Lazy Susan heard a peasant say, "I'm glad I'm not in King Swithbert's shoes right now. If *we* were glad she's been gone, think how happy he must have been without her."

"Come on, Mr. Lucasa," Lazy Susan said, grabbing a mule by the bridle. "Let's get out of this mob." She pulled the flowers from her hair so as not to be conspicuous. She didn't think the crowd sounded as welcoming as Olympia apparently did.

Together they located the stables and deposited the mules and the wheelbarrow with a bewildered stable boy, then followed his directions to the kitchens, where Mrs. Clover could be found.

Explaining what they were doing there took quite some time, as Mrs. Clover kept interrupting to say things like "Queen Olympia is really back? Oh, dear," and "Are you sure it's her? Couldn't there be some mistake?" and "Everything has been so lovely and calm here for the last year. Oh, dear."

Finally Lazy Susan was able to make her understand the situation—that she was meant to be Olympia's handmaiden, and that Mr. Lucasa was to work in the kitchen and with the chief seamstress.

So Mrs. Clover sent both of them off to see Sedgewick, the head butler, about getting the proper uniforms, and spent the rest of the day wringing her hands and fretting.

As Olympia mounted the staircase to the breakfast room, she felt quite pleased with the sensation she had caused in the bailey. How smart of her to arrive on Market Day. Making a dramatic entrance was important to maintaining one's image, and she thought she had done very well. The flowers and the mule had turned out to be brilliant elements—a touch of the commoner, but with a regal presence. Really, that entrance had had everything: surprise, drama, whimsy, pathos.

Swithbert waited at the top of the stairs. *Oh!* she thought, *he has that dreadful troll with him, the one who had been part of that melee at Marigold's wedding.*

What was he doing here? Why wasn't he in the

dungeon where he belonged? She could see that things had gotten out of hand in a big way since she'd been gone. But that was Swithbert for you. Too softhearted, and way too incompetent to be a decent ruler.

She held both her hands out to the king, ignoring Ed.

Swithbert had no choice but to take them. While he was normally gentle and good-hearted, at that moment he thought that a lot of trouble could probably be avoided if he just gave her a little shove down the stairs. He was immediately ashamed of himself.

"It really is you, isn't it?" Swithbert said. He'd been hoping she was an impostor, or a joke, or a nightmare. But face to face, he could see that it really was Olympia. A little worse for wear, to be sure, but there was no mistaking that cocksure gleam in her eyes. Or that ferret on her shoulder.

"I thought you'd be happier to see me," she said.

"I guess I'm—" he stammered. "I'm—in shock, I suppose. We all thought you were—well, you know."

"Dead. Yes, I know."

"Where have you been, then? Why didn't you come back sooner?" He wanted to withdraw his hands, but she had a vise grip on them. Involuntarily, he shivered.

"I lost my memory from the trauma of falling in

the river. But evidently I washed downstream to a little village called Granolah where I lived until I recovered my memory. They called me Angelica."

"*Angelica?*" Ed said. He couldn't help himself. "How on earth did they come up with that one?"

"Who asked you?" she said, turning her glare onto him. "For your information, they thought I was very sweet and kind. As indeed I am."

Ed stifled a snort.

"You do remember," Olympia said to him, "what the dungeon looks like, don't you?"

"It doesn't look like that anymore," Ed said. "It's a horse that's changed its spots. Now it's a storehouse."

"A storehouse? Storing something besides prisoners?"

"Storing my collections. I've been living here ever since Christian and Marigold got married and moved into my crystal cave in Zandelphia, turning it into their royal residence."

She narrowed her eyes. "Is that so? So she *did* marry him. Well, no one can say I didn't try to stop her."

"Nobody but you wanted that wedding stopped," Ed said. "Now Marigold is Queen of Zandelphia."

"I don't find that the slightest bit credible," Olympia said. "What does Marigold know about being a queen? The very idea is ridiculous."

"It's actually not," Swithbert said. "She's an excellent queen."

"You can believe I'll be checking into that. Well, there's plenty to do here at Beaurivage, I can see, before I take on anything with Marigold. But I can do that. It'll be fun."

*Not for everybody,* both Edric and Swithbert thought as they escorted Olympia into the breakfast room.

# 8

While Olympia, Ed, and Swithbert were out in the great hall at the top of the stairs, Christian had sat in the breakfast room, his head in his hands. In his misery, he had missed all the dramatics of Olympia's arrival. He'd also missed the departure of Ed and King Swithbert, so he'd kept talking to them, even when they were no longer there.

"This is the worst I ever felt in my life," he moaned. "Even worse than when I got shot with that poisoned arrow on my wedding day. Maybe that was an omen. Wedded bliss—ha! Marriage has a lot in common with having a poisoned arrow in your guts."

Then he raised his head and saw he'd been addressing an empty room—and he was glad. Until that morning, being married to Marigold *had* been completely like bliss, and nothing at all like being skewered by a poisoned arrow. But now he felt so awful, the only thing he could think of that would make him feel worse would be if Olympia came back. Thank goodness there was no chance of that ever happening.

MARIGOLD FINALLY raised her head and stopped crying, though the dogs continued to bay. Baying was fun as well as a way of sympathizing with Marigold.

*Bawling and feeling sorry for myself is no way to solve a problem,* she thought. She and Chris had both been childish and unreasonable that morning. Because that was so unlike their usual way with each other, they needed to talk about what had happened, and *now,* before the black mood that had taken them over got any stronger. She missed him too much already.

When a thorough search of the cave-castle didn't turn him up, one of the footmen remembered seeing him cross the bridge to Beaurivage Castle. Marigold ran to the bridge with the dogs on her heels.

AS SHE CROSSED through the bailey in Beaurivage Castle, there seemed to be an unusual amount of commotion for Market Day. The noise level was higher and the tone was more agitated. But she didn't stop long enough to overhear any of it. She had to find Christian and fix things.

She pushed through the crowd of marketers, entered the castle, and rushed up the staircase to Swithbert's breakfast room. She knew she was likely to find her father and Ed there at this hour, and they would know where Christian was. As she got to the top of the stairs, Bub and Cate came racing down the hall toward Flopsy, Mopsy, and Topsy, growling like tigers. They stopped, hackles raised and fangs bared at the smaller dogs, who snarled right back.

"Stop that! All of you!" Marigold ordered.

Of course they ignored her.

"Whatever disagreements you have among yourselves," she went on as she kept going down the corridor, "now is not the time to be airing them. We need to find Christian."

At his name, all the dogs abandoned their conflicts and jealousies and followed Marigold. When she opened the large carved door to the breakfast room, the dogs surged past her. They leaped on Ed, bringing him down in a pile of fur as they competed to get the blue squeaky toy, which they had all sniffed out and located in his pocket.

In the distraction of the dog attack, Marigold hardly registered who else was in the room. Once she knew that the dogs hadn't hurt Ed, she looked around and saw Christian (with relief), Swithbert (with affection), and Olympia—wait—Olympia?

"Mother," she gasped.

"Yes, it's me," Olympia replied. "Surprised?"

"That is hardly the word for it," Marigold said, having trouble catching her breath. For the last year she'd been fervently grateful that she'd never have to deal with Olympia again. She'd been so sure that the woman who'd made her life as Princess of Beaurivage so miserable, with her constant criticism, and punishments, and insistence on that horrible bow-laden wardrobe, was gone for good. Once Marigold had learned that Olympia was not really her mother—not even any blood relation at all—she had vowed never to refer to Olympia as her mother again. But shock and habit can make one do odd things. And now, here Olympia was again, a bad dream that didn't disappear upon awakening.

But Marigold had something else, something more important, to take care of first. Turning to Christian, she asked, "Are you all right?"

"No," Christian said. "My heart hurts."

Tears came into Marigold's eyes. "Mine, too."

Christian held his hands out to her. "I'm sorry. I don't want to ever hear you say that again."

She went into his arms. "Me, too."

Olympia cleared her throat. "Marigold!" she snapped. "That is no way to welcome your mother who was believed to be dead."

"You're not my mother," Marigold said, her voice muffled against Christian's chest. "I'm never calling you 'Mother' again. My real mother was a village girl whose name you never even bothered to remember. But even if I'm adopted, Swithbert has been my father in a way you never were my mother."

Olympia turned a basilisk glare at Swithbert. "What is she saying?"

"The truth," Swithbert said, sounding very kingly. "As you well know."

For once, Olympia was at a loss for words. But not for long. "Be that as it may, I'm the only mother she's ever known. And I'm the queen!"

"I'm a queen now, too," Marigold said. "I'm no longer the Princess of Beaurivage that you can push around. And unless you're even more self-involved and oblivious than I think you are, you must have noticed that no one seems especially glad to see you."

Although she was making this part up, Marigold

had always sensed the moods of Beaurivage in a way Olympia never could. And Marigold knew how the populace had felt about their queen. Oh, maybe there were a few subjects with extra-large hearts who would be happy she wasn't dead—but she couldn't think who they might be.

"That's a *lie!*" Olympia exploded. "Everyone in the market square shouted out my name in welcome. They've missed me. Even Swithbert missed me. Didn't you?" She turned to him.

"Hmmm," he said. King Swithbert was never deliberately unkind to anyone, even people he didn't especially care for. But he also tried to be scrupulously honest at all times. His dilemma was plain.

"*Didn't* you?" she insisted.

Marigold had to wonder why people sometimes did this—forced an answer out of somebody when it was clearly going to be something they didn't want to hear.

"I believe I missed what we might have been," Swithbert finally said. "But I missed that when you were here, too."

"Never mind," she said, dismissing him with a wave of her hand. "The important thing is I'm back. I get to be a queen again, and I'm starting right now. Get that troll out of here. He doesn't belong in Beaurivage. And

Marigold, if you're a queen the way you say you are, shouldn't you be in your own kingdom, taking care of your business, and not in mine, getting in the way? And you," she said, pointing at Christian. "I'm sure you should be somewhere else, too." She grabbed Swithbert by the upper arm. "You and I need to have a talk about whatever it is you've done to the north turret. It seems to be paved all over with tiny white bricks. Whatever possessed you to do such a thing?"

Swithbert yanked his arm out of Olympia's clutches. "Those are baby teeth, and I think they look quite beautiful. Like little pearls. Ed's business, Tooth Troll Limited, operates out of Beaurivage Castle now. It's been a source of revenue for us, with visitors paying to take tours of the tower."

"Revenue, you say?" Olympia looked thoughtful. "We could get more out of these visitors, I'm sure. Sell them honey tarts and marzipan and pheasant kidneys on a stick. Charge them to let their children wield one of our battle-axes or pet the unicorns. Sell them little replicas of the turret, or shirts embroidered with I SAW THE BEAURIVAGE TURRET OF TEETH."

"Oh, for goodness' sake!" Marigold said. "Come on, Chris. Let's go home."

"With pleasure," he said, taking her hand. They

departed together, leaving the dogs under the breakfast table quarreling over the blue squeaky toy.

"No, Olympia," Swithbert said. "We're not doing that. We're not turning this castle into some sort of— of BeaurivageWorld. We will continue to have a simple turret tour, for a small, reasonable fee."

The two monarchs faced off, and it seemed that a charge crackled in the air between them. Swithbert had rarely said no to Olympia before. And never before had she considered him any obstacle to doing exactly what she wanted. It was clear that something about Swithbert had changed. Something important. Olympia would bet anything that troll was behind this somehow. Which meant the troll had to go. And not just as far as the other side of the bridge, either.

And Marigold! Marigold, who had been nothing but trouble her entire life. In her youth, her troublesomeness had been manageable by punishments, threats, isolation, and swill (or nothing at all) for dinner. Now she was a queen in her own right, which would make managing her a bit more difficult. But definitely not impossible.

Olympia could see that a year's absence had caused them to forget just how commanding, how masterful, she could be.

"I need a bath," she said. "And some decent clothes, and a hairdresser, and a feast of my favorite things. Then I'll be ready to sit down with Rollo—he's still captain of the guards, I assume—and Sedgewick and Mrs. Clover and get this place straightened out."

"I'll call a maid for you," Swithbert said. "As for straightening this place out, I've been ruling alone for a year and I'm quite satisfied with the direction the kingdom is going. Rollo and Mrs. Clover and Sedgewick are not the ones you need to be talking to."

"We'll see about that," Olympia said, sweeping out the door and slamming it behind her.

"Uh-oh," Ed and Swithbert said at the same time.

As the queen headed down the corridor to her suite, she said to Fenleigh, "We have a lot of work to do, don't we? Won't it be fun? It'll be even more fun once I've eliminated Swithbert—and that troll, while I'm at it—and I'm sole monarch."

# 9

Olympia had her bath. Then she had her feast while wrapped in a dressing gown. And before her meetings with Rollo, Mrs. Clover, and Sedgewick, she summoned Lazy Susan and Mr. Lucasa to her dressing room to service her wardrobe.

"Ooooh," Lazy Susan said, examining Olympia's court dresses. "These are too gorgeous for words. All that silk and all those ruffles. All those bows and all that ermine."

Olympia pulled a dress off its hanger and threw it on the floor. "Completely out of fashion, I'm sure. And even if it isn't, I'm not about to be seen in a dress that's a year old. I'll need all new things. Immediately!"

Mr. Lucasa picked up the dress. "I can do something with this," he said. "The material is beautiful."

"Do whatever you want with it," Olympia said. "And this." She threw another dress on the floor. "And this, and this, and this—" She kept at it until they were up to their knees in discarded clothing. "Now *this* one," she said, indicating the single remaining dress, "was made for me to wear to the reception after Marigold's wedding. The reception I never got to because I fell in the river. So no one but the dressmaker and I have ever seen it. This one I can wear. Lazy Susan, you help me. Lucasa, you get busy with this other stuff." She kicked at the pile on the floor.

Mr. Lucasa gathered up as many of the gowns as he could carry and left while Lazy Susan stayed to help Olympia dress. This involved a lot of ordering about, complaining, shouting, one incident of hair-pulling and two slaps, all of the above delivered by Olympia. By the time the queen was finally dressed, coiffed, and perfumed, Lazy Susan was exhausted, sulky, and rebellious, and wondering again what had turned her sweet friend Angie into this selfish, demanding shrew. She had also just done more work in a single day than she had done in any previous year, and she hadn't liked that one bit, either.

"I'm going down to my meetings now," Olympia said grandly. "Be here when I get back to help me undress."

"Fat chance of that," Lazy Susan muttered as Olympia left the room. "Figure out how to get your own self out of that complicated monstrosity of an outfit." The simple life of Granolah, which had seemed so dull and repetitious when compared to Beauty's circumstances, now seemed almost unbearably precious. Oh, to sit on the stone bench by the well again, doing nothing but watching the village go by. To lie in her bed at midday resting from the rigors of eating breakfast *and* lunch. To have time to rehash her old resentments against Beauty. Though, at the moment, seeing what life in a castle could be like, Lazy Susan wasn't sure she was as envious as she used to be, no matter how handsome Beauty's prince was. Being a queen was apparently quite a strenuous job.

She headed for the small attic cubicle that Mrs. Clover had assigned to her, threw herself on the narrow cot, and was instantly asleep.

THAT NIGHT, no one slept soundly except Olympia— and that was only after the episode of bellowing when she discovered Lazy Susan was not waiting to disrobe her. Four other maids and seven footmen were sent to scour the castle, and Lazy Susan was delivered to Olympia just in order to be demoted to scullery maid.

Ed lay awake worrying that Olympia would find a way to dismantle his tooth-covered turret, or bring a halt altogether to Tooth Troll Limited.

Swithbert lay awake in despair at the prospect of life with Olympia again, just when he was finally getting used to the blithe feeling of life without her.

Bub and Cate lay awake, making plans to somehow get that blue squeaky toy all to themselves.

So did Flopsy, Mopsy, and Topsy.

Christian pretended to be asleep so he wouldn't disturb Marigold, but he worried for Marigold's safety. He hadn't forgotten that Olympia had once contemplated arranging a fatal accident to get Marigold out of the line of succession. Theoretically, as Queen of Zandelphia, Marigold was already out of the Beaurivage line of succession. But if Swithbert's plan for uniting the two kingdoms came to fruition, she would be back in it.

Marigold pretended to be asleep so she wouldn't disturb Chris, but she hadn't forgotten what Olympia had once planned, either.

Lazy Susan, having slept all afternoon, was wide awake, wishing she'd never had a friend named Angie.

And Mr. Lucasa stayed up all night making alterations to Olympia's gowns.

The next morning, Olympia was the only one of them whose eyes weren't bloodshot.

# 10

Magnus Tobias Hunter, who had been briefly engaged to Marigold before that crazy day when she ended up marrying King Christian of Zandelphia instead, was having a leisurely luncheon on the terrace of his country manor house. He could hardly believe how happy, and how lucky, he was. He had his own home at last, one that he'd designed himself to be exactly what he wanted. He had a job as royal architect and engineer, which had allowed him to make substantial improvements to the living conditions of Beaurivage's subjects. In just a year, this had made him so popular that, to his amazement, he'd won the annual Kingdom's Favorite Person Award. And that night Lord and Lady Buffleton, along with their daughter Sephronia, were coming to dinner.

Although Magnus had been willing to marry Marigold, he had mostly just wanted something he'd never had before—a place to belong. He liked Marigold well enough even though they had next to nothing in common. With Sephronia it was different. They always had plenty to talk about, and she even shared his interest in architecture and mapmaking. At tonight's dinner he intended to ask Lord Buffleton for permission to court Sephronia.

As he lifted his goblet of pomegranate juice to his lips, Magnus looked up to see something he couldn't believe. Queen Olympia appeared to be steaming across the terrace toward him, but that was impossible. While he'd been shocked at what happened to her on that wedding day a year ago, he couldn't say he was sorry. She had intimidated and manipulated and frightened him into a plot to do away with King Swithbert, and it had been the worst time of his life. She considered herself too refined to do any actual exterminating—that's what she wanted him to do. Magnus really loved Swithbert, who had never been anything but kind and generous to him, but he had been terrified of Olympia. He had been beyond relieved when she'd gone into the river, believing that she'd never bother him again.

Yet here she was, looking fit and extravagantly dressed, complete with ferret, and very much alive. His pomegranate juice went down the wrong way and he coughed so hard he saw stars.

"Just as competent as ever, I see," Olympia said, coming to a halt in front of his table while he kept trying to catch his breath. She yanked out a chair and sat down. "Nice little place you've got here, Magnus. A butler and all the trimmings. I'll bet Swithbert is behind your having it, am I right?" Without waiting for an answer, she said, "You were supposed to end up with nothing if you didn't marry Marigold. Which is exactly what would have happened if I'd still been around. But Swithbert . . ." She shook her head in disgust. "I'll bet you'd like to keep living in this nice place, wouldn't you?"

Magnus was too stunned to do more than look at her, his lips trembling.

"Of course you would," Olympia went on, reaching for Magnus's glass of pomegranate juice and drinking it down. "So I know you'll be glad to help me do what I want to do in exchange for your getting to stay here. Correct?"

"What—what—" Magnus licked his lips. "What do you want to do?"

"Ah, that's my boy," Olympia said. "Well, I want to be queen, of course."

"But aren't you queen now?" Magnus asked.

"Well, yes, technically. But the succession is through Swithbert. I was a commoner—though quite an uncommon one, I must say—when he married me. Succession goes to his offspring. Since Tatiana and Marigold are already queens of their own kingdoms, that leaves Calista and Eve, who tried being queens and didn't like it. And Swithbert would never make them do something they didn't want to do. So who better than me to succeed him? Once we get rid of him?"

It was Magnus's worst nightmare—she wanted him in on a plot to kill Swithbert *again*. In spite of his anxiety, a thought came to him. "Where have you been for the last year?"

"I can see I'm going to have to print my story in the *Daily Discourse*. I'm getting tired of explaining it." She sighed and summarized the whole thing for him in a singsongy voice. "Now. That's out of the way. Let's get back to business. Swithbert."

"Uncle Swithbert already has a plan for the succession," Magnus said hesitantly. "He wants to combine the kingdoms of Zandelphia and Beaurivage. Especially since the new Zandelphia-Beaurivage Bridge makes it so much easier to go back and forth now. And he wants Christian and Marigold to rule both kingdoms when he retires."

"There's a bridge?" Olympia was outraged. "I don't want a bridge! I want Beaurivage to be its own separate kingdom. *My* own separate kingdom. And if Swithbert's retiring, *I* should be first choice as ruler, not Marigold. One kingdom should be enough for her." Olympia stood and began pacing, with Fenleigh clinging to her shoulder. "Is this plan in writing yet? Is it official? Does anybody else know about it?"

"I don't know. I know he's mentioned it to Chris and Marigold, but I don't know if it's anywhere in writing."

"I'll just have to talk to him about that, then." She turned her hard eyes on Magnus. "And if he doesn't cooperate, I'll be back to see you." She turned and swept out, leaving Magnus in such a state of nerves and terror that he put his head down on the luncheon table and wept.

# 11

No, Olympia," Swithbert told her calmly. "Ed is not moving out. And we're not tearing down the bridge. And we will combine the kingdoms, if Chris and Marigold agree. And when I retire, you will not be my successor. But even if you're not queen then, you can still have a very comfortable life here at court." He hated to say this, but he couldn't bring himself to exile her. She was still his wife, after all. And he took any vow very seriously.

"I'm queen now, and I want to stay queen," she told him. "Beaurivage is *my* kingdom."

Why, he wondered, couldn't Olympia just be

satisfied with things as they were? She had so much to be grateful for, so much more than many others would ever have. Yet it was never enough.

"Are you forgetting that Marigold's adopted, and that her husband, in spite of his royal blood, managed to get himself lost in the forest years ago and was raised by that *troll*?"

"Olympia, that's enough," Swithbert said wearily. "I'm not changing my mind. Find a way to be happy now that you're back." He left the room.

"Oh, I'll find a way," Olympia said to the closed door. "But you can be sure it won't be your way."

SOMEHOW MAGNUS overcame the awful distress caused by Olympia's visit long enough to see to the preparations for his dinner with the Buffletons. Still, he was sweating profusely when they arrived, and so agitated he could hardly speak.

"Magnus," Sephronia whispered as they followed her parents into the reception room, "is something wrong? You don't seem yourself."

"I wish I wasn't myself," he murmured. "I wish I was someone who lived far away."

"Why, Magnus," Sephronia said, drawing back from him. "If you lived far away, you wouldn't be living near me. Is that what you want?"

"No! No, Sephronia! That's not what I mean. I just mean—oh, it's too complicated to explain."

"Don't even bother," she said huffily. "I think I understand. I thought it was me you were interested in, but I see you were just using me to get to my parents. Are you angling to design a villa for them? Well, go ahead. But be careful they don't find out how manipulative you are." She hurried ahead to join her parents, and spent the rest of the evening in a silent funk while Magnus struggled to make conversation with the very puzzled Buffletons, who had been expecting to celebrate their daughter's engagement over dessert.

Sephronia didn't even say good night to him. She simply stalked out to the Buffletons' coach while Lady Buffleton called after her, "Sephronia! Where are your manners?"

Her manners, apparently, also wished to be living far away. At least far away from Magnus.

After they had gone, Magnus sank down on the entry hall bench with his head in his hands and wept for the second time in eight hours.

OLYMPIA DIDN'T EVEN wait until lunchtime the next day.

Magnus was gazing without the slightest bit of appetite at the breakfast plate of pigeon eggs and summer berries that Winterbottom, his butler, had brought him. He heard the front door bang open, and then the door to his dining room also banged open. And there she was—his holy terror, his nemesis, his bête noire: Olympia.

He groaned.

"Does that mean you aren't glad to see me?" she asked gaily, pulling out a dining room chair and seating herself. "Surely not, when I'm the one who's going to make sure that you get to keep this pretty manor house." When he remained silent, she went on, "Don't you want to know more about what you have to do to make that happen?"

Dismally, he shook his head.

"Now, now, Magnus, don't be difficult."

Fenleigh crawled off her shoulder onto the table, where he went to work on Magnus's breakfast plate. He was particularly fond of pigeon eggs.

"All I'm asking," Olympia went on, "is for you to help me make sure neither Swithbert, Marigold, nor Christian gets to be ruler of Beaurivage instead of me. That's all."

He looked at her through bleary eyes. "I don't suppose you mean they'll be going on a nice long vacation."

She smiled. "I guess you could look at it that way. A kind of *permanent* vacation."

He shook his head, even as he knew what it meant for him. But he'd already lost Sephronia because of Olympia. What did the loss of his home mean after that?

"You're saying no to me?" Olympia asked, astonished.

This time he nodded.

"You're sure about that?" she asked, looking at him through narrowed eyes.

He nodded again.

She stood. "Come, Fenleigh." The ferret ran up Olympia's arm and wrapped himself around her neck. "Magnus, you're making things harder for me. You're going to be so sorry you did that."

"I know," he said miserably.

After she'd gone, he looked around his pretty dining room with its elegant proportions, tall sunny windows, and lovely pale green walls. How he would miss it when he went back to living with various relatives, none of whom would be especially thrilled to see him. But he'd been pushed around by Olympia before. He knew what that felt like, and he didn't ever want to feel so guilty and craven again, regardless of the consequences. And he would never forgive himself if any harm came to Swithbert, Marigold, or Christian.

He wished doing the right thing was always easy and painless, but it didn't seem to work out that way.

# 12

Chris and Marigold were exceedingly polite with each other, measuring their words carefully, monitoring their behavior so they wouldn't do anything to upset the other person. Neither of them wanted a repeat of the day they'd had their first argument, when they felt farther apart than when they had lived on opposite sides of the river. They were supposed to be each other's best friend—and best friends behaved better than they had that day.

Besides, they had Olympia to think about.

"She's up to no good already. I know it," Marigold said.

"No doubt about it," Chris said. "And I'm thinking she still wants to be the queen. All by herself."

"You think Papa and I are in danger again?"

"I'm sure of it. Especially once she finds out Swithbert wants to unite our two kingdoms. She's not big on sharing."

"We don't *have* to combine the kingdoms."

"That still won't protect Swithbert. Besides, I think combining the kingdoms is a good idea. Anything that unites people instead of dividing them seems valuable."

Marigold sighed. "I agree. So what are we going to do about her?"

"What about those pals of yours? Those elves and sorcerers and all? Can they help?"

"Hmmm. Maybe. I'll send out a few p-mails and see."

Then, because telling him jokes had been part of their getting to know each other, even though he didn't always think they were very funny, she decided to offer him one. "Christian, do you know how long Cleopatra lived?"

"Huh?"

"Cleopatra. Do you know how long she lived?"

"Uh—I don't know. Maybe forty years?"

"No, silly. The answer is, all her life."

"Oh. Is this one of your jokes?"

"You couldn't tell it was a joke?"

"I thought it was a real question. A serious question."

"You really couldn't tell it was a joke?"

"I told you I couldn't. Are you suggesting I'm stupid?"

"I just thought it was obvious."

"Obviously not."

"Are you saying I'm not a good joke teller?"

"I didn't say that. But joke telling *is* an art."

"And I'm not a good artist?"

"Well, I didn't know it was a joke, did I?"

"Maybe that's your fault, not mine."

And suddenly, they were back where they had been before, without quite knowing how it had happened. It was as if Olympia's return had brought poisoned air that invaded their brains and turned them into the worst versions of themselves.

Christian reached across the table and took Marigold's hand. "We have to stop this. We're supposed to be living happily ever after."

She clung to his hand. "Maybe this *is* happily ever after. Maybe happy people still have disagreements."

"I don't doubt that," Chris said. "But the ones

we're having are so stupid. Shouldn't we be disagreeing about more important things?"

"I think Olympia has something to do with it. I think during that year her memory was gone and she was somebody else—somebody nicer—all her bad qualities piled up and got stronger because she wasn't using them. Now she's taken them back and they're bigger and more forceful than they used to be, and they're loose in our air. It's like we're inhaling a little bit of Olympia's personality with every breath."

Chris cupped his hand over his mouth. "What a disgusting thought. But maybe you're right. That would make me feel better about these stupid arguments. I don't like thinking that we're being stupid all by ourselves, though I suppose that's possible. And if you're right, we're going to need some major help to get things back to normal."

"I'll get busy on those p-mails," Marigold said.

ED AND SWITHBERT sat in front of the fire, ignoring the fact that summer heat had arrived when Olympia had and a fire was unnecessary. There is something safe and comforting about sitting by a fire, and they needed to feel both.

"Olympia means to be sole ruler," Swithbert said glumly, mopping his brow with a handkerchief. "No matter who's in the way. Meaning me, and probably Marigold."

"What else is news to me?" Ed said, unbuttoning his jacket.

"I can't let that happen. It would be the worst thing possible for the entire kingdom."

"How you gonna stop her?"

Swithbert shook his head. "I don't know. I've never been good at stopping her from doing anything. She's like a charging bull. Or cow, I suppose. How do you stop one of those?"

"Spears. Arrows. Trip wires. Maces. Broadaxes. Cutlasses. Halberds. Pikes. Hatchets—"

"Okay, okay, Ed. But you know I'm not going to use any of those on her. I can't."

"Maybe we can find somebody who can."

"Oh, Ed. You don't mean that. Anyway, you know I can't do that, either."

"I'm not sure I don't mean it. But I get that you're a rock stuck in a hard place. Can't live with her, can't eliminate her."

"Things were so good while she was gone. If only we could figure out a way to make her go away once more."

"I could push her into the river again. I'd be glad to."

Swithbert sighed. "She's my problem, not yours."

Sedgewick came into the room. "Forgive me for interrupting, sire," he said, "but something odd is happening down in the dungeon. My, it's awfully warm in here." He wiped his brow with his green-trimmed hankie.

"What's happening in the dungeon?" Swithbert asked.

"The queen's ordered them emptied. All of Sir Edric's collections are being shoveled out of the cells and left in a disordered heap to be disposed of later."

*"What!"* Ed squealed. "Okay. Now she's *my* problem, too." He ran out of the sitting room and through the labyrinthine corridors of the castle until he came to the steep stone staircase that led to the dungeon. He'd spent some time in there, thanks to Olympia, so it seemed poetic justice (or prose justice, in Ed's mind) that he'd been able to store his collections there when he moved out of the crystal cave-castle so that Christian and Marigold could move in. He'd spent years accumulating those forest-found items and every one was precious to him.

He hustled down the steps yelling, "Stop! Stop!" even before he could see anybody doing anything.

In the dungeon four of Rollo's men were working away with big shovels, flinging Ed's carefully sorted items (one cell for left shoes, one cell for right shoes, one cell for forks, one cell for books, two cells for weapons, etc.) into one big pile at the darkest end of the dungeon's passageway. That was bad enough, but worse, he could see that the soldiers had helped themselves to some of the finest specimens, setting them aside to take away once the cleanout was finished.

"Stop!" he yelled again. And once again the soldiers ignored him. "Those are mine!"

"Not anymore," one of the soldiers said, flinging a shovelful right over Ed's head, into the messy conglobation beyond him.

"Why are you doing this? Those things have been there for a year."

"Queen Olympia's orders. She wants to use the dungeon again."

That was not good news.

Ed could see there was no stopping the soldiers, but at least he could stay and keep an eye on them so they didn't steal any more of what belonged to him. Well, it had belonged to somebody else once, but it belonged to him now.

Once the soldiers had finished and left, Ed cast a melancholy look at the mountain of his possessions languishing in the murky black hole of Beaurivage's dungeon, then went upstairs to tell Swithbert what was going on.

# 13

Lazy Susan sat stewing in the scullery. Waiting on somebody as bad-tempered and demanding as Olympia had been no fun, that was for sure, but scrubbing out kettles in which dragons' heads had been boiled was even less fun. Yet, she didn't want to go back to Granolah. Not without something to show for her stay in Beaurivage. It wasn't everybody who got to live in a castle and rub elbows with royalty. Lazy Susan wanted to be able to tell Beauty some stories about this adventure—and not just ones about being yelled at by Olympia, and about being up to her elbows in dragon fat.

She needed a better job.

Mrs. Clover came into the scullery and looked down at Lazy Susan sitting idly on a stool with her hands between her knees.

"How are those kettles coming along?" she asked pointedly.

"They're repulsive," Lazy Susan said.

"That's true," Mrs. Clover agreed. "But getting them clean is a necessity. And a great accomplishment. Something to be proud of."

"How would you know?" Lazy Susan muttered sulkily.

"Because that's how I started out here at the castle," Mrs. Clover said. "I was a scullery maid scrubbing out repulsive kettles."

"I don't believe you."

"It's true. Ask anybody."

"So how did you get to be head housekeeper? Who did you know who helped you out?"

"I didn't know anybody except the other scullery maids, and the footmen. But I worked hard and did the best job I could and didn't complain even when I was dead tired and my fingers were bleeding from the scrubbing. And the head housekeeper noticed. Somebody always notices when you're doing a good job, even if they don't say anything. They notice when you're doing a sloppy, haphazard job, too." And she indicated the kettle in front of Lazy Susan.

"What happens then?" Lazy Susan asked. She was experiencing an unfamiliar sensation. She didn't even know what to call it. Always before she'd been content to avoid effort of any kind, and she hadn't cared who knew it. But the things Mrs. Clover had said to her made her feel . . . maybe ashamed? Or chastened? Or embarrassed? Whatever it was, it wasn't a good feeling.

"Well, if you do a lousy job for long enough, what happens is, you get fired. Then you don't have a job. And most people need their jobs."

"I never have before."

"Why is that?" Mrs. Clover asked.

"Well—" Somehow now she didn't want to mention Beauty.

"Is it because you're Sleeping Beauty's half sister?" Mrs. Clover was smarter than you might think at first glance. "People do you favors because they think you'll get them in good with her and her prince?"

"I—maybe." She was regarding Mrs. Clover with new respect.

The housekeeper shook her head. "Poor Susan. Beauty is busy living her own full life and you're wasting yours. Don't you want a life of your own? One that's not stuck to hers?"

"Even if it involves a lot of dragon fat?" Lazy Susan asked.

"You can be sure there's something in your sister's life that's the equivalent of dragon fat. Maybe she hates formal dinners, or having to spend hours on harpsichord lessons, or embroidering with her ladies-in-waiting when she'd rather be outside digging in the garden in a simple country girl's dress. No matter how good somebody else's life looks from the outside, you can be sure there's something about it you wouldn't want to have in your own life."

Lazy Susan didn't want to believe this. She'd envied Beauty's circumstances for such a long time, she didn't like thinking that maybe they weren't so enviable, and that she'd wasted a lot of energy on something so unnecessary. But Mrs. Clover's words had been delivered with such surety that it was hard not to think there was at least *some* truth to them.

"But what you've got in your life right now," Mrs. Clover went on, "is a lot of dirty kettles. I'll leave you to decide what to do about them." And she left the scullery.

Lazy Susan sat, looking and deciding. To scrub dragon fat or not to scrub dragon fat—that was the question.

# 14

Mr. Lucasa delivered an armload of dresses to Olympia's quarters. He was met at the door by Miranda, who had been Olympia's personal maid before she'd floated down the river.

"She's on one of her rampages this morning," Miranda whispered. "You might not want to go in there. I can take the dresses if you want."

"My work," Mr. Lucasa said with a note of pride in his voice. "My rampage."

"Don't say I didn't try to protect you, then," Miranda said, opening the door wide.

Mr. Lucasa could hear Olympia before he could see her. He might not have been able to understand every word, but he definitely got the drift. She was mad at almost everybody for the way the kingdom and the castle had been run for the past year and she was going to fix things if she had to put half her subjects in the dungeon.

Miranda had been right to warn him, but she'd underestimated his ability to handle somebody having a tantrum. They just had to be ignored. It was so simple a tactic it's no wonder people didn't want to believe it; they persisted in thinking solutions needed to be complicated.

He took the dresses into her sitting room and began laying them out across the settees and armchairs while Olympia roared on to a cowering Sedgewick.

"And the gardens are a disgrace! There's scum in the reflecting pool, a blight on one of the rosebushes, and I even saw a unicorn loose in the orchard, eating the cherries right off the tree!"

"The pool was scheduled for cleaning last month, but it was raining, Your Majesty. And Razi loves cherries." Sedgewick quavered when Olympia stopped for breath. "The king said it was all right. He's so fond of that unicorn."

"And Swithbert!" Her voice went up a few more

decibels. "Why isn't he wearing his crown at all times? How is that incompetent valet Denby allowed to let him get away with looking like some old vagabond? You *are* head butler, you know. You're supposed to keep things running perfectly smoothly—and I can see that you haven't. You know I've had the dungeon cleaned out. There's plenty of room down there now."

Sedgewick gulped so loudly that Mr. Lucasa could hear him. He continued smoothing out the dresses. "I have your gowns," he said quietly.

"Can't you see I'm—" Olympia looked sharply at the array of finery. "Those are *my* gowns? The ones you took away a few days ago?"

Mr. Lucasa nodded.

She came over to inspect them, fingering the new trimmings, checking how the necklines had been altered and the skirts draped. "This sleeve," she said. "It needs to be an inch shorter. And this waistband— too wide. And . . . uh . . ."

He could tell she was looking for something else with which to find fault and failing.

"Who helped you with these?" she finally asked. "I'm quite sure it wasn't that do-nothing Lazy Susan."

"Mrs. Clover sent me to Mrs. Vienna."

"She's the chief seamstress now," Sedgewick put

in timorously. "She's new since you . . . left, Your Majesty."

"And she helped you?" Olympia asked Mr. Lucasa.

"No. I did it all. She just gave me the supplies."

Abruptly Olympia turned to Sedgewick. "Go! Get that unicorn back in its stall! And see that the reflecting pool is cleaned out! And rip out that blighted rosebush." She pointed to a dress. "Give me that one. I'm going to try it on."

Mr. Lucasa handed her the gown, and while she and Miranda were in the dressing room, he wandered around the sitting room looking at the paintings and statues and ornaments and carvings. There were lots and lots of them. Some were fine and beautiful, and others were garish and ornate. Olympia seemed to want everything, without any kind of discernment, just to have it.

"Well?" she asked when she came back into the room.

He examined her silently for a moment, and then said, "Here." He touched one shoulder. "And here." He indicated a seam on the bodice. "I'll fix those. Try another one."

At the end of an hour, Olympia had tried all the gowns and was impressed at Mr. Lucasa's creativity and attention to detail, though she certainly wasn't going to tell him. To her way of thinking, praise made people slack and shiftless (except for herself, of course, for whom there was no such thing as too much praise). It took criticism, and plenty of it, to keep people performing.

# 15

Swithbert and Ed rode out into the countryside on Razi and his stablemate Petunia for one of their regular visits to Magnus. As they rode along, they had the odd feeling that they were being followed. But every time they turned to look, they saw nothing but the trail, surrounded by the trees of the forest.

At Magnus's manor house, they banged on the front door. Winterbottom ushered them in, saying, "I'll see if Sir Magnus is up yet."

"Up?" Ed said. "It's afternoon. Is he sick?"

"Ever since the queen was here, he's taken to his bed. I'd say he's sick in his spirit, thanks to her." Then he remembered who he was talking to and added,

"Begging your pardon, sire. I meant no offense." He, too, had heard that the dungeon had been reopened.

"Never mind that," Swithbert said with a sigh. "I'm afraid I know too well how she can have that effect. But I didn't know she'd been to see Magnus."

After Winterbottom had gone upstairs, Swithbert said to Ed, "You know, she used Magnus before, when she was trying to get rid of Marigold and me. I wonder if she's recruiting him again. If she is, I know just what she'd threaten him with."

"His house," Ed said. He knew how that could feel. He'd voluntarily given his crystal cave-castle over to Marigold and Christian. After all, it *was* in Chris's kingdom of Zandelphia, and it *was* just across the river from Swithbert's castle, and Chris *had* grown up there, and it *was* beautiful enough for a royal residence. But sometimes he wished he hadn't. After all, he *had* lived there for over one hundred years, and he *did* have all his collections stored there, and he *did* love the place more than anywhere else he'd ever lived. He knew you couldn't cross back over a burned bridge when you came to it, as the saying went, but some days, much as he'd liked living at Swithbert's, he wished he had his own place again.

After a long while Magnus, in his dressing gown, came draggling down the stairs behind Winterbottom.

"Hello, Your Majesty. Hello, Ed. I beg your pardon for my appearance. I'm a little under the weather."

"Yes, I can see that," Swithbert said. "And I have an idea of what's wrong with you."

Magnus gave him a startled look. "You do?"

Winterbottom herded them into the sitting room. "I'll bring tea," he said.

"So . . ." Magnus hesitated and then tried again. "What do you think is my problem?"

"Could it be—Olympia?" Swithbert asked.

Magnus went paler than he already was. "Did she say something to you?"

"No. But I know her. I know how she operates. And I know what she did to you once before."

Magnus hung his head. "I shouldn't have cooperated with her then. But I was younger, and a little desperate, and—"

"It's all right, Magnus," Swithbert said. "I understood."

Magnus raised his head and looked at the king. "I really did like Marigold. But I knew all along we had nothing in common."

"I know. What you wanted was a place to belong. I really do understand that. Which is why I made sure you got your own house. And now . . . I'm just guessing, but could it be that Olympia's threatening to take that away from you unless you do what she wants? And what she wants probably has something to do with my health, just like last time. Am I close?"

Magnus jumped. "How did you know?"

Swithbert shrugged. "Unfortunately, I know Olympia."

"But this time I told her no. I swear it."

"I believe you. And that's why you're so under the weather. Wondering what her retaliation will be. I'm sure you've heard she's cleaned out the dungeons, ready for business again."

Ed jumped in. "We aren't ones to want to wash our dirty hands in public, so we'll need to keep this conversation confidential. But we have to stop Olympia."

"Do you think we can?" Magnus asked doubtfully.

"That's what we need to talk about."

So they did, spending a long time over the tea and cakes that Winterbottom brought. Ed was especially fond of the raisin scones and ate more than he should have. Trolls have very little restraint when it comes to food they love.

Swithbert ate modestly, mostly because that was his usual practice, but also because he had had such perfectly boiled eggs for breakfast that he'd requested them again for lunch and was quite full still. Either the old cook had finally learned how to boil an egg properly, or someone else had taken over the job.

Magnus was too upset and bilious to eat a bite.

AT THE END of the afternoon they'd gotten exactly nowhere. Every plan they came up with had holes even they could see through, which meant it wouldn't have fooled Olympia for an instant.

"It'll be dark before we return to the castle if we don't leave now," Swithbert said. "But we'll keep racking our brains about Olympia, and we'll meet again tomorrow. We must solve this problem before it goes any further."

Ed opened the door to the sitting room and found Winterbottom on the floor, held down by Rollo's boot in his back, and with Rollo's saber poised at the nape of his neck. An eight-foot-tall captain of the guards is intimidating under any circumstances, but especially when he has his blade on one's neck.

"Rollo!" Swithbert commanded. "What are you doing here?"

"I've been eavesdropping all afternoon," he said. "I and two of my archers followed you. Queen's orders. And she's not going to like what I have to tell her."

"Olympia's had you spying on us?" Swithbert asked in astonishment.

"For good reason, apparently," Rollo said. "The three of you are under arrest."

"Me?" squeaked Winterbottom from the floor. "All I did was make tea. And more raisin scones than I thought anybody could eat. But he did." And he pointed a finger at Ed.

"Not you." Rollo removed the saber. "Him, and him, and him," he said, waving the blade at Ed, Swithbert, and Magnus. "And I can promise you, there won't be any raisin scones where they're going."

"I need to get dressed," Magnus said, looking down at his bare legs, slippers, and dressing gown. "I can't go anywhere like this."

"You think I'm simple enough to let you go where you could escape or fetch a weapon?" Rollo scoffed. "You're coming just as you are."

# 16

It was a pitiful little procession that Rollo and his archers escorted back to the castle in the twilight. A storm was brewing off to the west, and the rumble of thunder and flash of lightning accompanied Ed (his stomach aching from all the scones), Magnus (struggling to keep his dressing gown closed while on horseback), and Swithbert (fighting back tears at his own failures).

The downpour started just before the entourage reached the castle, and by the time Ed, Magnus, and Swithbert were locked into separate cells in the dungeon, they were dripping wet and shivering.

"When will we get our trial?" Swithbert asked. "It's

in the Beaurivage constitution that everybody accused of something gets a trial."

Beaurivage was unusual because it was a constitutional monarchy. Most monarchies operated at the whim of the monarch; Beaurivage had rules. But Swithbert had a sinking feeling about Beaurivage's famous rules just then. Olympia had never been fond of rules—unless they were her own. And if she were sole monarch, there would be plenty of whims.

"I guess you haven't heard," Rollo said. "The queen is rewriting the constitution."

"But it says in the constitution that no single person can do that," Swithbert protested. "There's a process that has to be followed."

"That was the first thing she changed," Rollo told them, and left them in the dankness of the dungeon.

The king slumped down against the damp cell wall. "Can you ever forgive me for getting you all into this?" he called to Ed and Magnus. "It's completely my fault. I should have been able to manage Olympia on my own."

"Nobody can manage her on their own," Magnus called back, and sneezed.

"At least it's clean in here," Ed said rather dolefully, since the cleanliness reminded him that all his precious possessions were gone. He paced around his cell in the guttering light from the torch stuck in a bracket on the corridor wall. He found, overlooked by the cell shoveler-outers, a bent fork and a gold button. Not much help there.

They were silent, each trapped in his own gloomy thoughts, until a commotion on the stone stairs leading down to the dungeon roused them from their funks. They were all standing at their barred cell doors when Olympia came sweeping along the corridor with all the trappings of royalty and then some—crown, ermine cape, scepter, orb, ropes and ropes of pearls, diamond-studded badges, emblems, and brooches pinned to her dress, feathers and ribbons attached here and there, and an escort of four soldiers carrying standards with her coat of arms on them.

She stopped in front of his cell. "Hello, dear," she said coldly.

"Hello, Olympia." Swithbert, with effort, kept his voice level.

"Got yourself into a spot of trouble, I see."

He was silent.

"And your friends, too," she went on. "A shame to have brought them into this. Now you'll all be guilty of treason."

"Guilty?" Swithbert said. "We haven't been tried yet."

"Oh, what's the point of a trial?" she asked airily. "Why waste everybody's time? I have a lot to do to get this kingdom on its feet again. No time for such nonsense."

"Fairness is hardly nonsense," Swithbert said. When she only glared at him, he swallowed hard and said, "Is there—is there a sentence?"

"I'm still thinking about that," Olympia said, tapping her chin with an index finger almost covered by a huge ruby ring. "I can't decide which would be more satisfying, and instructive to my subjects—a public hanging, or a lifetime in here following a public flogging. I really do need to make an example of you, just so I don't have any more of this kind of trouble. I'm sure you understand."

A wretched croak came from Magnus's cell. Olympia turned to him. "I'll bet you're wishing you hadn't said no to me when you had the chance to say yes. Am I right?"

He cleared his throat. "I'm not sorry I said no," he rasped. "But I am sorry to be in here."

She laughed gaily. "I only give one chance, anyway, so you'd have ended up here no matter what." Turning to Ed, she said, "And *you*. You escaped from here once before, but I can assure you, that won't be happening again."

"Don't be so sure about that," Ed said defiantly, though he had no idea what he might do about it.

"Oh, I'm sure," Olympia said. "There'll be a guard here night and day until I decide your fate." She spun on her stacked red heel and swept back to the stairs waving her fingers at them. "Ta ta, now."

There was a long silence as they watched the guard take his post, standing at stiff attention, pike in hand. Finally Ed muttered, "This is a fine kettle of hen's teeth."

As the hours wore on, Ed, Swithbert, and Magnus could only fret and doze and shiver. Soon the guard, whose name they learned was Finbar, was shivering, too, and trying hard not to doze. Guarding innocent people isn't very interesting—though technically, of course, they were *very* guilty because they *had* been plotting against the queen.

But some plots are necessary, and even required.

# 17

Marigold spent the day writing p-mails. She'd had to do some hard thinking about who to send them to. It's true she wanted Olympia stopped, and preferably sent far, far away. But, in spite of the dire fate Olympia had planned for her and for Swithbert, she couldn't bring herself to ask someone to do the same to Olympia. She had to phrase her request very carefully—and in three to six lines, since each pigeon-leg capsule could hold only a short message.

She finally settled on:

> *Have you any interest in helping me*
> *rid Beaurivage of a dangerous queen?*
> *No bloodshed, please.    —Marigold*

She sent the pigeons—Walter, Carrie, and their offspring—into the sky, carrying the messages to various carefully chosen fairies, sorcerers and sorceresses, witches and warlocks, wizards and shamans. Then she settled down to wait.

She paced. She overwatered her plants. She threw the ball a thousand times for Flopsy, Mopsy, and Topsy (all of whom kept wishing it was the blue squeaky toy). She picked her cuticles and ate a lot of chocolate and looked at the sundial eighty-seven times in a single hour.

It was nearly dusk when the first pigeon returned. Marigold almost broke its leg trying to get the message cylinder off, after which the pigeon stalked away to its perch, exhausted and pouting.

The message read:

> **Sorry. No bloodshed, no interest.**
> **Love, Morven**

She threw the message onto the floor and paced some more.

In the next hour, six more pigeons returned, all carrying variations of Morven's message.

*When did everybody get so bloodthirsty?* Marigold

wondered. Didn't any of them have enough imagination to figure out how to eliminate Olympia without such conventional and gory methods?

Overnight several more pigeons trickled in, ones who had been unable to find their addressees, or who brought back rejections—too busy, too uninterested, or too retired. Only Carrie remained unaccounted for, and Marigold was fearful something had happened to her. She was getting a bit old for much long-distance work, though she was always eager to go. Marigold had deliberately given her the closest assignment, and still she hadn't returned.

Finally, late the next morning, Carrie arrived, bright-eyed from a good night's sleep, plump from a scrumptious dinner and breakfast, and proud of the answer she brought. Wendell the wizard had agreed to help. He would be arriving in Zandelphia in a few days to discuss details.

Then Marigold paced some more. She'd almost left Wendell off her mailing list because of his advanced age and his reputation for incompetence. But once, when he had visited Swithbert when Marigold was a little girl, Wendell had been very kind to her, doing magic tricks to amuse her, pulling candies from her ears and coins from her empty pockets. She'd never forgotten that, as most visitors to the castle had been so dazzled by her beautiful blond triplet sisters that they completely ignored her. She had p-mailed him mostly as a courtesy, never dreaming he would be the only one to offer assistance.

When she told Chris that Wendell had agreed to help them, he looked up from a sketch of a new invention and said, "Are you sure that's a good idea?"

"No. But everybody else has turned us down. They're only interested if they can spill blood." She shuddered.

"Olympia had no qualms about plotting to spill yours," Chris reminded her.

"I know. But emulating Olympia isn't something I'm interested in doing. Wendell's been around for a long time. Maybe he's got some ideas that'll work."

"What if you don't like his ideas? Are you willing to peeve a sorcerer? Even an old one past his prime? He could probably still set you on fire, or turn you into a rabbit."

"Please, Chris. I'm nervous enough without your making things worse."

"I'm just trying to be realistic. Don't get your undies all in a bunch."

"I beg your pardon?" Her tone was icy.

"You know what I mean," he said absently, fiddling with his sketch.

"You think I'm overlooking important parts of our plan to neutralize Olympia? Or you think I'm over-reacting?"

He looked up. "Huh?"

"Never mind," she said. "I can see I'm on my own here." And she left the room.

"What?" Chris said, watching her go. "What did I do now?"

But there was no answer. Probably just as well.

THE NEXT FEW DAYS passed v-e-r-r-r-y, v-e-r-r-r-y slowly for Ed, Swithbert, and Magnus in the dungeon. They passed slowly for Finbar, too, who was bored almost beyond endurance from watching them sit listlessly in their cells.

The days passed very, very fast for Olympia. She had so much to do: rewriting the constitution, having fittings for all the new gowns she'd commanded Mr. Lucasa to make, mulling the sentences for Ed, Magnus, and the king, and haranguing every servant in the castle about their sloppy job performances.

The days passed very busily for Mr. Lucasa; very uncomfortably for Lazy Susan, who couldn't stop thinking about what Mrs. Clover had said to her; and very impatiently for Wendell the wizard as he made his way slowly to Zandelphia.

The days passed very nervously for Marigold as she waited for Wendell to arrive, and very lonesomely for Christian, to whom Marigold was not speaking.

# 18

In the middle of the sixth afternoon of waiting, the gate guard at Marigold's cave-castle came running into the throne room where she sat, chin in hand, drumming her fingers on the arm of her throne.

"Your Highness," he panted, "there's a great white beast coming across the bridge with a little old man in a purple robe on his back! Shall I call out the archers?"

Marigold stopped drumming and sat bolt upright. "It's Wendell! Show him in as soon as he arrives. And get some refreshments up here, something really luscious. Make sure his elephant is well taken care of, too."

"Uh, how does one take care of an elephant?"

"I have no idea. Ask Wendell what the elephant needs."

"Who *is* Wendell?"

"The wizard who's riding the elephant, of course," she said impatiently. "Now hurry!"

The gate guard hustled off, his nose seriously out of joint. Queen Marigold had never spoken to him like that before. She hadn't even said "please" or asked him how he was, or about his wife and kiddies. Come to think of it, King Christian hadn't been himself for the past few days, either. He'd seemed preoccupied and rather downcast, not even saying "good day," the way he usually did when he passed a servant. The gate guard had worked for Queen Olympia before Queen Marigold, and he had been so thankful to get out from under Olympia's thumb that he still said a little prayer of gratitude every day. But now he was wondering if Marigold had inherited some of her mother's imperious manners, and he just hadn't noticed until now.

WENDELL WAS USHERED into the throne room, dusty and thirsty from his long trip. Marigold rushed to greet him, a goblet of cold checkerberry juice in her hand.

"I'm so glad to see you," she exclaimed, hoping

that she actually would be. "Thank you for coming all this way."

"I try never to ignore a damsel in distress," he said, handing her a little rectangle of cardboard.

"What's this?" she asked.

"My invention. I'm calling it a business card."

She examined the card.

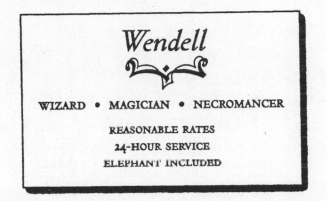

Wendell

WIZARD • MAGICIAN • NECROMANCER

REASONABLE RATES
24-HOUR SERVICE
ELEPHANT INCLUDED

She knew having one of those saved a lot of explaining—because Magnus had already invented them. But she wasn't going to spoil Wendell's pleasure in what he thought was his own concoction. She needed him to feel clever and innovative.

"This is a great idea," she said. "So practical. But what's a necromancer?"

"Somebody who gets information about the future from those who have already departed this realm."

"You mean died?"

"Well, yes."

"You can really do that?"

He gulped down the checkerberry juice and held his goblet out for more. "Not yet, to be honest. But I expect to soon. I'm working on my technique. Now, tell me what's on your mind."

"Wait. First I need to know about your reasonable rates." She refilled the goblet.

"Oh. Well, usually it's a firstborn child—"

"What!" Marigold almost dropped the pitcher. "You call that reasonable?"

Wendell hung his head. "You're right. Nobody else thinks it is, either. So far I haven't collected a single one. But it *is* the traditional price. And I need to ask it if I'm going to be taken seriously as a wizard."

"You mean all wizards ask that price?" Marigold was aghast. Without this information she might have made a deal with somebody who wasn't nearly as malleable as Wendell—if she'd been willing to go for the bloodshed—and then she'd have been expected to pay up. Now she was thinking that sometimes things work out the way they're supposed to, even if at first it seems like they haven't.

He nodded. "They all do. I'm not sure how many of them get it. Lately I've heard some of them are asking for other things, so maybe that's more modern, and I'm just behind the times." He brushed some dust off his shoulders.

"What kind of other things?" Marigold asked. She didn't want any more surprises.

"Oh, sometimes an arm and a leg. But mostly just gold, jewels, or animals. That makes more sense as far as I'm concerned. Who really wants a bunch of other people's firstborns to take care of? Especially since us wizards do so much traveling. Or a pile of severed limbs, either. What good are those?"

"It makes more sense to me, too," Marigold said, relieved.

"Why don't you tell me what's going on?" Wendell said, gazing hungrily at the spread of delicacies laid out on the sideboard.

"As soon as you've had a snack," Marigold said graciously.

While Wendell piled his plate high, he asked, "Should we wait for your husband, the king, before we start?" She was quiet for so long he wasn't sure she'd heard him.

Just as he was about to ask again, Marigold replied, "No. That won't be necessary. I'm handling this myself."

Wendell seated himself and began chowing down while Marigold explained the situation with Olympia.

Wendell cogitated. "How about if I just vaporize her? Poof her off into some other dimension."

"Can she still do any harm from there?"

He rubbed his chin. "It's not unheard of. If there's enough bad energy hanging around her, she might still be able to use it—the part left behind—even if she's not here in person."

"Oh, there's plenty of bad energy. More than enough to keep operating long after she's gone."

"All right, then, that won't work." Wendell looked worried.

"Isn't there some way to make her be nicer without hurting her, or doing something bad to her?"

He scratched his head. "That would take some stronger magic than I know how to do. Being nicer has to come from the inside, not the outside. That requires a complete rearrangement of everything inside the head. And the heart. And so far nobody's cooked up any kind of spell or potion to do that. Maybe someday—" He sighed and then said, "Until then, the best we can do are immobilization spells, or vaporizations, or outright explosive eliminations. Any of those appeal to you?"

She shook her head. "Not really. But we have to stop her somehow before she ruins her kingdom and makes everybody in it totally miserable. And that's not even counting what might happen to my father, the king. And to me, too."

"What do you mean? It sounds like you think you and the king are in danger from her. Is she that wicked?"

Marigold hated to use that word, but she couldn't think of one that fit better. "I guess so," she said in a tiny voice.

"This is serious," Wendell said. "I'm pretty good at making flowers grow faster, or snow fall in summer, or clothes change colors, but real evil—that's beyond magic. That takes something else."

"What? What does it take, then?"

He scratched his head and thought hard. Then he said, "I don't know. People have fought it for a long, long time, and it's still around. Sometimes it's a little quieter, but it always comes back."

In a whisper Marigold asked, "So what are we going to do?"

He took a deep breath. "I can keep working on my necromancy. Maybe at least I can have a look at the future for you. See what happens to the kingdom. That might give us a clue as to what Olympia's going to do."

Marigold had no confidence that Wendell could do that. But she knew it would be rude to send him away so soon after he'd arrived, so she resigned herself to having him around for a few weeks, accomplishing nothing. After all, she'd asked for his help and it wasn't nice to turn him away just because he couldn't give her what she wanted.

If only all she wanted was a quick, clean vaporization. Or a dramatic (though probably pretty messy) explosion. She knew it was fruitless, and unrealistic, and plain silly besides, but what she really wanted was for Olympia to just be somebody else.

# 19

Christian was surprised to see Wendell at the dinner table that evening.

"Nobody told me you'd arrived," he said, sliding a reproachful glance in Marigold's direction. "That must be your elephant out there in the stable, making the unicorns nervous."

"That's Hannibal, all right," Wendell said. "He's gentle as a puppy. Wouldn't hurt anybody except by accident. He just doesn't quite realize how big he is." Wendell was hard to understand because he was stuffing food in his mouth with both hands, as if he hadn't had a sumptuous repast just a few hours before. "Hannibal's worst problem is how opinionated he is.

If he doesn't want to go, he doesn't go. If he wants to go right when I want to go left, we go right. If he doesn't like somebody, he just picks them up with his trunk and shakes them."

"I thought you said he was gentle as a puppy," Chris said.

"Oh, he wouldn't hurt anyone. But sometimes a good shake is all it takes to turn somebody around."

Marigold put down her fork. "Do you think that would help with Olympia?"

Wendell shook his head. "It works for unpleasantness. Not true evil."

"Oh." She took up her fork again, only to pick indifferently at her dinner.

The rest of the meal was silent except for the sound of Wendell chewing. This kind of silence was unnerving to the servants, who were used to how lively their king and queen had once been—how much they had to say to each other, how much fun they had, and how many jokes Queen Marigold told. Something was definitely wrong in Zandelphia, and they hoped the wizard wasn't the one who was expected to fix it. Along with his atrocious table manners and his disreputable appearance, he didn't look as if he could magic his way out of a paper bag.

Christian excused himself as soon as he'd finished eating, saying he had to get back to work on an invention. That left Wendell and Marigold looking at each other across the table.

Wendell, also sensing something wrong in Zandelphia, ransacked his mind for a way to cheer Marigold up. "You know, I've heard you like jokes," he said. "The last kingdom I was in had just developed a new kind of joke you might be interested in. It's called a knock-knock joke and it takes two people."

"Knock-knock?" she asked, interested. "You mean the way you would knock on a door?"

"Yes, exactly. I'll tell you one. Your part is to say, 'Who's there?' when the knock comes. Ready?"

"All right. Go ahead."

"Knock, knock."

"Who's there? Is that right?"

"Yes. Good. Now I answer you. I say, 'Shirley.'"

"Hmmm," Marigold said. "That's supposed to be funny? I don't get it."

"We're not finished yet," Wendell said, trying not to sound impatient. This kind of joke was so difficult to explain, he was wondering if it would ever really catch on. "When I tell you who's there, you have to say, 'Shirley who?'"

"Oh. Well, then, Shirley who?"

"Shirley you know who this is," Wendell said triumphantly.

"Yes, I do," Marigold said. "It's you."

"No, no. That's part of the joke." And then he had to explain what the jokey part was, knowing that when you do that, the joke is a failure.

"Can we try that again?" Marigold asked. "I'm not sure I understand how it works yet."

Wendell sighed. "Knock, knock."

"Who's there?"

"Shirley."

"Shirley I know who this is," Marigold said. "It still doesn't seem very funny."

"You left out a step." He explained the process to her again, and said, "Let's start all over with a different joke. Remember, you say 'who's there' when I say 'knock, knock,' and you say 'who' when I tell you who's there. Ready?"

"Ready," Marigold said, and sat expectantly on the edge of her chair.

"Knock, knock."

"Who's there?"

"My panther."

"What!" she exclaimed. Did he have a panther as

well as an elephant? But after a sharp look from Wendell she remembered, and said, "My panther who?"

"My panther falling down."

"My panther . . . ," she mused. "Oh! My *pants* are falling down!" And she laughed and laughed, the way she hadn't for days. It felt so good. "Oh! I *love* knock-knock jokes! Tell me more."

So they sat together telling jokes while the servants stood restlessly around, waiting for Marigold and Wendell to leave so they could get on with clearing the dishes. Finally they ran out of jokes and went off to bed, with Wendell exhausted after his long trip and the effort of entertaining the young queen, and Marigold in better spirits than she had been in for several days.

By the time Marigold fell asleep, Christian had still not come in from his workshop. And she'd tried so hard to stay awake so she could tell him this new kind of joke. Even when things were tense between them, he was still the first person she thought of when she wanted to share something.

CHRISTIAN HAD been working on a miniature trebuchet. He'd wanted to surprise Marigold with it at breakfast, catapulting an orange from his end of the table to hers. But now he was afraid she wouldn't think it was funny. Now she'd probably think he was attacking her. How things between them had gotten to this point, and in such a short time, was impossible for him to understand—unless it was because Olympia's malevolent energy had been set loose in the kingdom again. He needed more than a miniature trebuchet to fix that. If only he had one big enough to land a boulder on Olympia and eliminate the problems once and for all.

He was immediately ashamed of himself for thinking such a thing about the woman who was, after all, his mother-in-law.

OLYMPIA DECIDED a trial *was* necessary for Swithbert, Ed, and Magnus. If she was going to be sole monarch she didn't want her subjects thinking she was an irrational cutthroat. She wanted them to know she was a responsible ruler. One who could be benevolent (when she felt like it, which was rare) and fair (when it suited her, which was hardly ever), but who would not tolerate treachery and disloyalty (ever).

Besides, she knew that Swithbert and Ed, and even Magnus, were held in fond regard by the Beaurivageans. In order to expose them for the doubledealing, two-faced rats and traitors that they were, she had made sure that all the details of their crimes were being circulated through the kingdom's gossip grapevine. A trial would put the finishing touch on them, and head off any kind of grassroots movement to salvage their popularity.

There weren't going to be any uprisings or peasant revolts in *her* kingdom.

# 20

D o you think Olympia's going to have us killed?"
Magnus was pressed against the bars in his cell, calling to Swithbert.

Swithbert shot a glance at Finbar, and then decided that it probably didn't matter *what* he had to say
about Olympia. He was sure she'd already publicly
branded them as traitors and made up her mind about
what she would do with them, and it almost certainly
wasn't going to be fun. For them, at least.

"I can't say no to that," he said. "She's wanted to
get rid of me for years. And as long as she regards you
and Ed as my friends, and equal impediments to what
she wants, well . . ."

Magnus gathered his dressing gown around himself in the chill, and slunk back to the corner of his cell. He should have known things were going too well: his new house, his popularity, Sephronia. Nothing in his life had ever worked out for the best for very long. He'd been stupid to think it would now.

"Stop beating around the handwriting on the wall," Ed piped up from his cell. "We know what she's going to do. What we need to do is get down to brass monkeys and stop her from doing it."

"Good idea, Ed," Swithbert agreed. "*How* would be the question."

"Oh, yeah," Ed said, also slumping back into his corner. "You're right. Do you think anybody can get us out of here? Anybody like Marigold or Christian, who might—"

Swithbert interrupted. "Don't count on it. Olympia doesn't want any interference with this endeavor of hers. Knowing her, she's made it clear that she's in charge of Beaurivage now. And she definitely wouldn't welcome any meddling by somebody from another kingdom."

"You got that right," Finbar put in. "She's been gone so long I'd almost forgotten, but that's how she does business. Like the way she sprung that engagement between you"—he indicated Magnus with his pike—"and Princess Marigold at that dinner just three days before she wanted to have the wedding."

Swithbert, Magnus, and Ed could only figure that Finbar had become so bored he had to have somebody to talk to, and they were the only candidates. Swithbert made a little signal to Magnus and Ed to keep quiet as he said to Finbar, "Yes, the kingdom was a different kind of place while she was gone, wasn't it?"

Finbar got a far-off look on his face. "Aye. That it was. Us guards were all getting to relax a little, without worrying she'd make us do something we didn't think was right. She was always having me kick somebody out of the castle in the middle of the night for doing nothing more than dressing some way she didn't like, or singing off-key. She's a hard dame to please."

"You're telling me," Swithbert said. "Tell me, Finbar. You seem like a discerning fellow. Do you think the citizens of Beaurivage are happy their queen is back?"

Finbar gave Swithbert an incredulous look. "Only if they like living in fear all the time again." Then he seemed to remember who he was talking to and what his job was. He straightened up. "But she's back, and she's the queen, and she says you're all traitors. She gives the orders, and I follow them."

"Not long ago, I was the one giving the orders," Swithbert said a bit wistfully.

"Yeah, I know," Finbar said, softening slightly. "And believe me, I don't like being the guy who has to be guarding you."

"Do you believe her, Finbar? Do you believe I was plotting treason against her?"

"Well, if you weren't, you should have been," Finbar said, indignant. "You're the *king*! You could have stopped her before she got started again. When you didn't do that, you made things harder for all your subjects."

"And for myself and my friends, too," Swithbert said sadly.

"Maybe you deserve it, then," Finbar said, throwing back his shoulders and standing at attention again. He'd worked himself up into a fit of righteousness and made Swithbert even more miserable than a person already locked in a dungeon awaiting who-knew-what awful fate should feel.

APPARENTLY MRS. CLOVER was going to leave Lazy Susan in the scullery with the dirty kettles forever. Each day Lazy Susan was sent back in with her scrubbing brush and her bucket of hot water. And each day she sat on her stool while the water cooled, and the servants brought in more pots caked with dragon fat, stuck-on nightingale feathers, and baked-on hoofen-poofer juice. Surely they would run out of pots in the kitchen soon, she thought, and then somebody—somebody besides her, that is—would have to come in and clean them.

Looking at the piles of pots and kettles gradually crowding her into a corner of the scullery was making her more and more uneasy. If she was ambitious, the way Mrs. Clover had been, perhaps she'd have gone right to work scrubbing. Or if she was trying to please someone or earn her keep, she'd have set to work. But she was none of those things.

Still, the sight of all those dirty pots, disgusting and revolting as could be, was making her feel she should do something about it—as if the pots had begun to regard her reproachfully, and even somewhat sadly, at how she was neglecting them. Too, she had to admit, spending hour after hour just sitting there staring at them was supremely boring. Back in Granolah she'd been perfectly capable of spending hours lying in a hammock watching the activities of the village, having a vicarious sense of participation. But here there was nothing going on she could pretend to be a part of. Any activity would have to be one she generated herself. Was she willing to have that activity be pot scrubbing?

MR. LUCASA HAD plenty to do. He'd never worked for a more demanding person than Queen Olympia—or one who changed her mind more often. He'd ripped off and sewn back on the same band of fabric roses five times on the same dress. First she liked them on the shoulder, then she didn't. Over and over again. She appeared to operate under such a head of steam it seemed impossible that she could keep up that pace. Sometimes he even thought he could hear infuriated thoughts whirring and clanking in her skull, and if he could look inside her ear with a good strong light he imagined he'd see machinery operating at such a wicked speed that it would be smoking.

Still, he liked the work he was doing, playing with fabrics and trimmings and solving puzzles of construction. Even more, he liked working in the kitchens, where he was part of a creative team. He especially liked making cakes and pastries, where he could let his imagination loose. His desserts often turned out like fanciful architectural structures, or replicas of everyday items that looked so real it was hard to tell the difference from the actual thing.

One day he'd watched the royal dogs fighting over a single blue squeaky toy. So he'd made five little cakes, each shaped like that toy, and presented them to the dogs. They'd been ecstatic—until the cakes were consumed. Then they'd gone back to fighting over the real blue squeaky toy. But Mr. Lucasa had been pleased that his creations had been realistic enough to keep them from fighting, even if only for a short time.

That was the day Olympia almost had the dogs kicked out of the castle to live in the stables, she was so sick of hearing them fighting. But when she came out of her suite, they were all peacefully lying on the carpet in the corridor, chewing. So she swept on by, confident that her reprimands had finally had some effect. And she had much more important problems on her mind than a few dogs.

# 21

With Christian occupied in his workshop and Wendell shut up in his room working on his necromancy, Marigold was at loose ends. She couldn't concentrate on any book, her interest in developing a new fragrance wandered, and Flopsy, Mopsy, and Topsy had run across the Zandelphia-Beaurivage Bridge to play with Bub and Cate at the castle. Though, come to think about it, they all hadn't been getting along so well lately.

Well, maybe she'd go across the bridge, too. She'd avoided visiting since Olympia had returned, for obvious reasons, but she hadn't seen her father for over a week and she was missing him. She wasn't going to allow Olympia, whatever schemes she might be hatching, to intimidate her from seeing her father—and from making sure he was all right. It was true she'd had to wait around at home for Wendell to show up, but now it was a sure thing, she was afraid, that she wouldn't be missed if she took the afternoon off and left the castle. Chris seemed barely to notice her even when he was in the same room with her.

She wondered if this was the way every marriage ended up, especially royal ones: suffocated by obligations and formalities. She and Chris had even talked about that on their honeymoon and promised not to let it happen. But maybe it was inevitable. It didn't seem to have happened to her sisters, those beautiful blond, impossibly lucky triplets, all of whom had married royalty, but they had been extraordinary and fairy-blessed all their lives. They weren't like anybody else, so she couldn't use them as a gauge of anything.

She set off across the Zandelphia-Beaurivage Bridge. She couldn't help admiring it every time she saw it. It reminded her again and again of how clever and brilliant Chris was to have designed such a beautiful, and also tricky, structure. A bridge like that made both kingdoms feel safer when invaders could be dumped into the river with the operation of a few gears.

She entered the bailey in the midst of a throng of peasants arriving for Market Day. Rollo had pulled aside, and was threatening, a farmer who wanted to bring in more than his allowed number of pigs, all squealing and scuffling about in the farmer's wagon. Rollo seemed unfriendlier than usual. Maybe his mood had something to do with his having to work for Olympia again. She could be a tough boss even if you agreed with her about everything, which Marigold supposed Rollo did. You probably didn't get to be captain of the guards by differing with your queen.

As Marigold made her way through the castle courtyard she thought she sensed anxiety in the crowd: a discontent, or unease, or even foreboding. Or maybe she was just projecting her own feelings—about Chris, about her abilities to rule wisely, and especially about what Olympia could do to everything Marigold cared about. She reminded herself to be vigilant and wary, for herself *and* Swithbert, as long as she was inside Beaurivage Castle.

When she reached the top of the winding staircase in the south turret, where her father's private quarters were, she was surprised at how quiet everything was. Usually Swithbert could be heard playing with Bub and Cate, or enjoying a game of snipsnapsnorum with Ed, or reading aloud to one of the courtiers' children, or even just having a chat with Denby, his valet. But even after she'd knocked on the door, there was silence. Where was Denby? Where was the king?

She pushed open the door and went into the apartment. The sitting room was perfectly tidy and completely deserted. So was the bedroom. As she turned to go, she heard a sound from the dressing room—the sound of a snuffle.

She crept up to the door, pressed her ear against it, and listened. Someone inside seemed to be crying. She tapped on the door and the sound stopped abruptly.

"Who . . . who is it?" a watery voice asked.

"Denby?" Marigold said. "Is that you?"

The door opened and Denby stood there, red-eyed and pasty-faced. "Princess. I mean, Your Majesty," he gulped. "Sorry. I still think of you as the little girl who lived here."

"What's wrong, Denby?" Marigold asked. "Where's Papa?"

Tears welled in Denby's eyes. "I don't want to tell you."

Marigold made her sternest face. "You'd better," she said. "Remember, I have the imperial power of life and death." She doubted he would believe that she would harm him, but his lifelong habit of obedience to sovereign commands might work in her favor. And it did.

"All right, then. Queen Olympia has thrown him in the dungeon along with Ed and Sir Magnus. She says they're guilty of treason, and of plotting to depose her. Oh, I suppose that's the treason part. Anyway, right now she's deciding when's the best time to stage their trial. But of course she's already decided they're guilty, and a trial will just be for show. Today would have been a good time, actually, since it's Market Day and many of the farmers and peasants are already here at the castle. They could witness it and carry the news home with them."

Marigold's voice rose two octaves. "That means she's going to have them executed! Denby, we've got to get them out! How long have they been there?"

"It seems like forever." His eyes filled again. "But just about a week, really." He inhaled on another big sob.

"Well, don't just stand there. We've got to *do* something."

"Don't you think I've spent the last week trying to figure out what?" Tears streamed down his cheeks.

"You should have come to me first thing! I can get Chris to demand their release!" Marigold declared.

Denby shook his head. "I couldn't come to you. Every time I try to leave the castle, a guard stops me. In fact I'm surprised the queen hasn't prevented you coming in. She knows you'll be a complication."

"Nobody noticed me. Rollo was arguing with a farmer about some pigs."

"Oh. Well, anyway, King Christian could demand their release in his own kingdom, but not in somebody else's. I'm sure you can guess how the queen would react to being told what to do by somebody with no authority to do so. Which would be everybody except her. He'd end up in there with them."

"Then we have to break them out ourselves! We can hide them until we figure out what to do."

Denby was shaking his head again. "There's no way we can even get down there. She's got the door to the dungeon locked, and only she and the daily household guard carry the keys. And there's a guard posted right outside their cells so nobody can get close enough to talk to them."

"Well, *think*, Denby." She made a few little frustrated whimpers. "*Think!* We can't let this go on!"

"What do you suppose I've been doing?" he asked, rather snippily, she thought, but then decided she couldn't blame him. He was as frightened and as helpless as she was. "I can't come up with anything that could work. That's why I was crying in the dressing room."

Marigold gave herself a mental shaking. She had to remember that she was a queen, not a child terrified of her parent. And that Denby was looking to her for guidance. She patted his shoulder. "Poor Denby. This has been just awful for you, I know. I'll have to talk to the king—*my* king, I mean. Maybe he'll be able to think of something. I'll be back as soon as I can. Stay here."

"I have to," he said mournfully. "She won't let me leave."

Her heart pounding with desperation, Marigold held back her own tears and ran down the stairs so fast she almost took a header. Just as her feet went out from under her, she felt strong arms catch her. She looked up into the ruddy-cheeked face of a man wearing a white toque on his head of unruly white hair. At his feet was a basket filled with keys.

"Oh," Marigold said, righting herself. "Thank you. Who are you?"

"My name's Stan Lucasa," he said. "I'm new here. Are you, too?"

"Oh, I don't live here. Anymore. I live across the river." Her curiosity got the better of her. "What are all those keys?"

"They're my job today," he said. "The queen wants me to figure out which keys lock which doors. She's all upset because the king quit using the keys and let everybody come and go as they pleased. And now that he's been deposed, or whatever you want to call it, she wants to be able to lock people in again. I swear," he said, taking a couple of keys out of his pocket, "these don't seem to fit anything."

The idea that Olympia wanted to lock people in their rooms, the way she'd done to Marigold so many times in the past, made her just furious. She grabbed the keys from Mr. Lucasa. "And they won't," she said. "I won't let them." She pushed past him to go on down the stairs, but more carefully this time. "Thank you again for saving me," she said.

Mr. Lucasa removed his toque and, looking after her, scratched his head. "This is the oddest place I've ever been," he said as she vanished from his sight. "And she seems *nicht alle Tassen im Schrank haben.*" Which is German for not having all her cups in the cupboard.

# 22

Marigold hardly ever interrupted Christian in his workshop, but this emergency definitely qualified as an exception. She could tell he was surprised to see her, but she couldn't tell if he was pleased. However, once she'd begun explaining what was happening, he dropped everything and listened hard.

"You know I don't have any jurisdiction in someone else's kingdom—except for being intimidating—and I don't think that'll work with Olympia."

"But we have to do something! We can't let her execute them. Just come with me to Beaurivage. Maybe we can find a way to get to them."

Chris was dubious about that, but he didn't want

to risk starting another fight. So he hung up his tools and followed her.

As they crossed the pink crystal room, which had been converted into the main hall for the cave-castle, they crossed paths with Wendell, who was also rushing from his quarters.

"Oh, good," he said. "I've got something to tell you."

"Not now," Marigold said, tugging Chris along by the hand. "We're in a hurry."

"Oh, but this is important," Wendell said, rushing along with them. "It's about the necromancy. I think maybe I'm getting the hang of it."

"Good, good," she said without stopping. "That's wonderful."

"I mean," he said, panting slightly now, "I think I received a message. It might be for you."

Marigold stopped so suddenly that Christian bumped into her. "What? What do you mean? Why do you think it's for me?"

Wendell stopped, too, his hand on his chest while he tried to catch his breath. "Or for King Christian," he panted. "I'm not sure. I just got this—this *message* in my head. It just arrived there while I was working on something else. That's the way great ideas happen, don't you think? They just *come*. Anyway, it didn't seem to apply to me, so I surmise it's for one of you since I'm in *your* castle, and I'm here to help with *your* problem."

"Tell us!" Marigold and Christian cried together, curiosity warring with their need to get going.

"Well, let me see then." Wendell rummaged in his many pockets until he came up with a crumpled piece of paper. "Ah. Here it is." He adjusted his glasses on his nose. "Oh, no, wait. This is my dry cleaning ticket. I forgot to pick it up." He rummaged some more, and came up with another piece of paper. "Here. Oh, no, this is my grocery list. I was completely out of capers and maraschino cherries. Ah, here it is. It says, *The coming month will bring winds of change in your life.*"

"You think that's for me?" Christian said. "It could be for anybody. Even you. Everybody's life changes in some way from month to month."

"Oh," he said. "I suppose you're right. It does sound a bit like something from a fortune-teller. Does it ring any bells for you?" he asked Marigold.

"Not a single tinkle," she said, pulling on Christian's arm.

Wendell scratched his head. "Dang! Now I remember where I heard that. From a gypsy at the crossroads on my way here. It *was* just cheap fortune-telling, not necromancy. Sorry." As he wandered off, they heard him mumble, "Why can't I get the hang of this stuff?"

"Keep working on it, Wendell," Chris said. "Now we really have to go. We'll see you later." And they rushed off to Beaurivage.

THIS TIME, however, Rollo was paying attention and wouldn't allow them to cross the drawbridge into the castle.

"Orders from the queen," he told them. "You no longer have free passage. She says you're to stay in your own kingdom and mind your own business. Those are her words, not mine." He seemed a little embarrassed, but adamant.

When an eight-foot-tall person says you can't come in, the sensible thing to do is to go away. Which is what Chris and Marigold did. There are occasions when insisting on your prerogatives, royal or not, is just a waste of time.

As they walked away from the castle, Chris said, "I was tempted to try to get by him but I knew that wouldn't work. And then I was tempted to pull rank on him. After all, I'm a king myself." He always sounded a little surprised when he said that. "But I know Rollo's not easy to intimidate."

"But Papa!" Marigold exclaimed. "And Ed and Magnus! What are we going to do?"

They stopped in a little copse of trees to mull this over.

"Is there any other way in?" Chris asked.

"We could scale the bluff from the river up to the terrace with ropes, I suppose, but I'm not sure we're strong enough to accomplish that. I haven't been doing my weight-lifting exercises diligently enough lately. Besides, somebody would probably see us. The flying machine was never repaired after it crashed on the terrace on our wedding day, so we can't use that." She sat on a stump, her chin in her hand, her brow furrowed, and thought while Chris watched her.

Suddenly Marigold sat up straight. "There's a door! A little door right at the water's edge that opens out from the dungeon. They used it in the olden days to dump the torture victims into the river." She shivered at the thought. "It hasn't been used since long before I was born, though Olympia would threaten me with it when I'd been bad. But it might still work."

He grabbed her hand and yanked her to her feet. "It's our only chance. We have to try. Our fathers are in there."

# 23

They made their way through the woods around the castle until they came to the river's edge. Scrooching down the steep, muddy bank to the narrow strip of beach, Marigold lamented (but only for a moment) what was happening to her cute little beaded shoes. What were shoes, even cute ones, compared to the life of someone she loved? They were a worthy sacrifice. She hoped they would be the only one.

The curtain wall of the castle soared high above them, and plunged straight down into the riverbank. Moss and lichens covered the wall higher than their heads, and looked altogether quite slimy and vile.

"There's a door under this stuff somewhere?" Chris asked. "Are you sure?"

"Are you doubting me?" Marigold asked. "I told you it's here."

"Okay, okay. Don't get your—" and then he thought better of what he'd been about to say. He knew now where a remark like that ended up, and he didn't want to start that again with Marigold. "I mean, then let's find it."

She took a deep breath, and put her hands on the slick, mossy wall, feeling around for the edges of a door. "Ick, ick, ick," she said. But she kept groping through the gloppy growth. So did Christian.

"Hey!" he called after a while. "I think I've found a hinge." He scraped away a thick layer of moss with his fingers. Marigold hurried over to help him, and before long they had revealed a door with an iron ring mounted in the center.

"Pull it," Marigold said. "The longer we're out here, the more chance there is that someone'll see us from up on the terrace."

"You and your father spent more time out there than anybody else ever did," Chris said. "And I ought to know. I put in a lot of hours watching you through my telescope." He gazed down at her, remembering

149

that sweet and nervous time when he was first falling in love with her.

She gazed back at him, remembering the first p-mail message she'd received from him, when she'd been convinced that she'd be lonely for the rest of her life. And then he'd come along, first with his friendship, then with his love. How could she ever be irritable with someone who had changed her life? What came over her that caused her to speak to him the way she sometimes did?

Christian had turned back to the door and was tugging on the iron ring, to no avail. "This door is stuck, or locked," he said. "I can't get it open."

"Pull harder," she said. "I'll help."

But the door remained stuck shut.

When they stopped to rest, shaking out their cramping arms, Marigold had a sudden thought. "Maybe it's barred from the inside! Then we'll never get in!"

"We're not giving up yet," Chris said. "It hasn't been opened for a long time. It could just be rusted closed. We need something to pry it with."

"Why didn't you bring something?" she wailed. "You've got a workshop full of tools over there." She pointed across the river to Zandelphia.

He was about to snap, "Well, I didn't know I'd

need a workshop full of tools, did I?" but changed his mind in a hurry. He took her stiff body into his arms and said, "I know you're scared and upset. I am, too. But we need to be calm and sensible. So let's think a minute about what we can do."

He could feel the tension leave her as she brought her arms around him. "You're right. I'm so scared I can't even think. Thank you for being my bulwark once again."

For a while they just stood holding each other, feeling the double beat of their hearts, being afraid together.

Then Christian raised his head. "You know," he said, "that door has a keyhole in it. Maybe it's locked."

"Then it might as well be barred. We can't unlock it without a—" Then Marigold remembered the two oddly shaped keys she'd taken from Mr. Lucasa. Digging in her pocket, she pulled them out. "Here."

Christian took them. "Where did you get these?"

"From some fellow in the castle. I'll tell you later. Hurry! Try them before somebody sees us down here!" She was so anxious she was jumping up and down.

The first key wouldn't even go in, much less turn. But the second one slid right into the lock and turned easily. "Well, how do you like that?" Chris asked in amazement.

"I like it a lot," Marigold said, grabbing the iron ring. Chris grabbed it, too, and together they pulled the door slowly open. Luckily the rush of the river was loud enough to drown out the prolonged squeal of rusty hinges.

Inside was a long dark tunnel with a flickering light at the end of it. For a few scary moments they just looked down the tunnel, not knowing what they'd find, or whether they'd ever be coming out again.

Then they took deep breaths and straightened their backs. They had a job to do, and there was no getting out of it.

"Wait," Chris said, putting his arms around Marigold. "Before we go, I just want to be sure you know that I love you."

Tears swam in Marigold's eyes. "Oh, Chris. I do know that. We've been having a sort of bumpy time lately, but I really do know that."

"Good. We can talk some more about the bumps when we get out of here, but right now we need to move."

"All right. But you know I love you, too, right?"

"Right." He kissed her, and they stepped through the doorway into the fetid air and slime of the tunnel.

# 24

Finbar was leaning against the wall dozing when he heard a voice in his ear say, "Sit down on the ground and keep quiet."

His eyes snapped open to reveal two mud-covered figures, one of whom was holding Finbar's own pike pointed directly at his midsection. "Who?" he mumbled. "What?" He cast a quick glance at his prisoners, to find them with their hands over their own mouths to keep from making any sound that would have awakened him.

"Where, why, and when should be the next questions, I believe," Chris said. "But never mind all that. Give me the keys to the cells."

"Are you kidding? I'm the guard here. I can't do that."

"Then I have no choice," Chris said.

Chris removed a set of handcuffs from a hook on the wall and brandished the pike while Marigold fastened Finbar's hands behind his back. Hanging on the same hook was a ring of large keys, which Chris appropriated.

"One of those is for the door at the top of the stairs," Swithbert said. "The rest are for the cells."

"And still hanging in the same place as when I was a prisoner here," Chris said. "Doesn't Olympia know that cleaning out a dungeon every now and then isn't enough? Once in a while a dungeon has to be brought up to date, with all the latest improvements. Such as a new hook for the keys."

He tossed the keys to Marigold, who went from cell to cell, unlocking the doors. When she got to Swithbert's, she stuck the key in the lock and said, "Hi, Papa. You didn't think I'd let you stay in here, did you?"

"I didn't think you'd even find out I was here until it was too late," he said, and his voice quavered.

Marigold jiggled the key in the lock. She joggled and twitched and wiggled the key around, but the lock wouldn't open.

Ed and Magnus tried the key, too, but they couldn't get the tumblers to move, either. And the other key Marigold had taken from Mr. Lucasa was way too big.

While everybody's attention was focused on Swithbert's predicament, Finbar began scooting on his bottom toward the curving stone stairs that led out of the dungeon. He'd made it up the bottom step before Chris turned away from the lock problem and spotted him.

"Oh, no, you don't," Chris said, grabbing him by the ankle and pulling him back down onto the dungeon floor.

"Ow!" Finbar yelped as his head hit the bottom step. "That hurt."

"Sorry," Chris said. "But you know we can't let you get out of here to warn the guards. Jailbreaks work better without an audience."

"Not having much luck with this jailbreak, are you?" Finbar said, struggling without success to get to his feet.

"We'll get it done, don't worry," Chris told him. At that, Ed went back into his cell.

"Ed, what are you doing?" Chris asked. "The point is to get *out* of here."

"Keep your horses on," Ed said. "I'm just getting

something." He brought the bent fork from his cell over to Swithbert's, where Magnus was wrestling with the key with his right hand, and trying to keep his dressing gown closed with the other. "Let me try this," Ed said.

Magnus moved aside, and Ed began fiddling with the lock by sticking a tine from the fork into the keyhole. His brow puckered in concentration for a few moments, and then he said, "I'm not a Jack Frost of all trades for nothing."

The door to Swithbert's cell swung open and the king stepped out.

"Good man!" he exclaimed, clapping Ed on the shoulder. "I'd want you with me in any spot, but I'm especially glad you were with me in this one."

Ed beamed and looked down at his shoes. "I was just lucky," he mumbled, grateful that the meagerest remnant of his precious collection had still been useful.

Chris squatted down by Finbar. "See? We got it done."

"And now what?" Finbar asked. "Are you going to take on all the castle guards?"

"Maybe we won't have to," Swithbert said. "Maybe some of them would like to join us."

"Join you in what?"

"I'm taking this kingdom back. Ed and Magnus and I *are* traitors. We want Olympia off the throne."

"Nobody can stage a revolution alone," Chris said. "Us monarchs have to stick together. I'm in."

"Me, too," Marigold said.

"Me, too," Magnus said.

"Me, too," Ed said.

"Me, too," Finbar said.

They all looked down at him.

"I can help. I can keep quiet that you've escaped. I can get weapons. I can recruit revolutionaries from among the other guards."

"Are you sure you just don't want those handcuffs off?" Swithbert asked, sounding very kingly and in charge. "Are you sure you won't just go straight to Olympia and tell her what's going on?"

"Well, I *would* like to get the handcuffs off, that's for sure," Finbar said. "But I'd also really like to see you back on the throne, Your Majesty. Beaurivage was a better place when you were, no matter how peeved I am about the way you let the queen push you around. And I know it's important to do more than just complain when there's something you don't like. You need to try to do something about it, or you're nothing but a whiner."

"Well stated, Finbar," Swithbert said. "Maybe I could take a few backbone lessons from you."

"That's the only lesson I've got, what I just said." Finbar's voice sounded a bit strangled from his awkward position on the floor.

"Do you think Rollo would help?" Swithbert asked.

"Rollo!" Marigold and Christian said in unison.

"Rollo stopped us at the drawbridge," Marigold said. "That's why we had to come in through the old disposal tunnel."

"And Rollo hates me," Chris said. "He has from the first minute he ever saw me."

"And he threw me and Bub and Cate into this same dungeon and ransacked all my treasures when I still lived across the river," Ed said.

"What makes you think Rollo would want to help?" Magnus asked.

"I'm just asking," Swithbert said. "If he'd be with us, we'd barely need anybody else. He's big and he's influential. Nobody wants to argue with him any more than they want to argue with Olympia. *And* he's captain of the guards. They'll do what he tells them to do."

"Most of them, I think," Finbar said. "But like it or not, Olympia does have her followers—mostly other ferret fanciers, but they'd support her. A revolution always has two sides."

"Yes, that's true," Swithbert mused. "We need to get a reading of who would join us and who wouldn't. And none of us can go out into the castle and ask."

"There's a new maid," Finbar said. "She arrived with Olympia. Maybe she'd help us."

"Olympia's own maid?" Ed yelped. "Have you lost your crackers? Who'd be more loyal than her own maid?"

"No, wait," Marigold said. "Finbar's got a point. Who would know her better? Especially after many days of traveling together? Who would have plenty of reasons for mutinying after all that time being bossed around by her? But how to get to her, that's the question."

"Last I heard, she'd been sent down to the scullery," Finbar said.

Chris's eyes narrowed. "You seem to know an awful lot about this new maid. You wouldn't be trying to set us up, would you? Betray us?"

Finbar blushed and shook his head.

Marigold had to giggle. "It's simpler than that, Chris," she said, taking his hand. "I'll bet she's pretty. Right, Finbar?"

"Pretty enough," he said gruffly. "For someone her age."

"See, Chris? It's more about Finbar's eye for the ladies than about treachery. And I think the fact that she's in the scullery is a good sign. That means Olympia is displeased with her. So this maid—what's her name, Finbar?"

"I heard her called Susan. Lazy Susan."

"Why, that's Sleeping Beauty's half sister! I've heard of her. She has a big reputation for laziness. We're going to need somebody who's willing to really pitch in, not just stand by watching."

"How are we going to find out if she's up to it?" Magnus asked. "None of us can go upstairs."

"I can," Marigold said. "Look at me! I'm barefoot and filthy, and my hair's a mess. Nobody would guess for a moment that I'm me. I look like I belong in the scullery and nowhere else."

"Oh, precious," Swithbert said. "It's much too dangerous. Olympia would know you no matter how dirty you are."

"What are the odds Olympia'll be hanging around the scullery?" Marigold asked, wiping her hands across the floor and rubbing even more dirt onto her cheeks.

"Your father's right," Chris said. "It's too dangerous. I'll go."

"Don't be silly," Marigold said. "No scullery maid is going to spill her deepest thoughts to anybody but another maid. Especially not on short acquaintance, which this will definitely have to be."

"Marigold is right," Magnus said with a sigh. Even though he'd been sure he and Marigold would be badly matched as spouses, he had no doubt that she was smart and brave and knew what she was talking about.

"She is," Finbar concurred. "Queen Marigold is the one who has to do it."

"There, then, it's settled," Marigold said, with a surge of exhilaration that she had rarely felt before. One that came from knowing she was doing something important, no matter how it turned out. "I'll be back as soon as I can. In the meantime, just in case Olympia comes down here, the rest of you should maybe pretend to still be locked up."

"What about me?" Finbar asked. "How convincing am I going to be as a guard if I'm lying on the floor with handcuffs on?"

"He's got a point," Marigold said. "You all work it out. I've got to get going."

They watched as she took the key for the dungeon door, ran lightly up the stone stairs, and disappeared around the curve. They heard the creak of the great iron door as it opened, and then the sound it made as it closed behind her.

For a long moment there was silence as Chris, Magnus, Ed, Swithbert, and Finbar continued looking at the stairs, as if willing her back. Then Chris cleared his throat and set about unlocking Finbar's handcuffs.

FORTUNATELY FOR ALL OF THEM, at that moment Olympia was not thinking about the dungeon at all. She was sitting at her gilded writing desk working on the speech she would give to the citizenry on execution day.

Perhaps that was not so fortunate, after all.

# 25

Marigold crept along a passageway, hoping she wouldn't run into anyone. She'd spent a lot more time roaming around the castle when she was a little girl than most princesses did—out of curiosity mainly, but also because hardly anyone had paid much attention to her. Consequently, she knew the back ways and secret accesses to every part of the castle—including the scullery.

She came out through a little-used doorway that led to the farthest-away storage rooms in the bowels of the castle. That passageway was so seldom used that there was an inch of dust on the floor. Marigold tiptoed through it, glad to add another layer of grime to her disguise. She slipped through the back door to the scullery and stood still, holding her breath.

Luckily, there was so much noise that her entry went unheard. Before her was the backside of someone bent over a kettle so deep that the person was almost all the way inside it, scrubbing away with a brush so apparently big and bristly that it was banging on the sides, setting up a din that, under other circumstances, could have been interpreted as music. A continuous moaning reverberated inside the pot, a sort of singing sound to accompany the scrub-brush timpani.

After a few more minutes the banging and the moaning stopped, and the bottom backed out of the kettle. Attached to it was a woman covered in dragon fat and soapsuds. She threw down the brush and dropped onto a stool, her head in her hands. Then she shook herself, straightened her shoulders, and looked up.

When she saw Marigold, she uttered a squawk. "Where did you come from? Who are you?"

Marigold said casually, "Who do I look like? The queen?" Then she laughed. "I'm supposed to help you in here."

"About time," Lazy Susan said. "Now that I've almost got these things finished."

"You've scrubbed all these yourself?" Marigold

looked around at an accumulation of sparkling pots. She really was surprised, considering all she'd heard about Lazy Susan's work ethic.

"All except those three "

"That's a lot of scrubbing. Why didn't you have some help?"

"Ask old lady Clover. All this hard work was her idea. I've been sitting in here for days while the pots piled up. The only way I could get a little space for myself was to wash some so they'd come take them away."

"You mean you've been *living* in here?" Marigold was shocked. Such mistreatment would never happen in the castle of Zandelphia!

"Well, almost. I get out for meals, and to sleep at night. But the queen assigned me to this job, so I get put in here every morning. And every morning there have been more pots."

"There are a lot of people to feed here. That means a lot of cookware," Marigold said, almost apologetically. She inspected a kettle. "But you've done a great job. This is spotless. And I've heard hoofenpoofer juice is really hard to get off."

"How'd you know there was hoofenpoofer juice on that?"

"Oh, there's hoofenpoofer juice on almost all the pots. Everybody likes it, but especially King Swithbert.

He's always had to have at least one serving a day." It made her very sad to think of her poor father in the dungeon with none of his favorite treats.

"You really think that pot looks clean?" Lazy Susan asked.

"Absolutely. I don't know how you did it."

"Lots of scrubbing, that's how. And some spit helps, too, I discovered."

"Spit?" Marigold wondered if she'd ever want to eat hoofenpoofer at Beaurivage Castle again.

"Oh, I washed it off, but it seemed to make it easier to get the stuck-on stuff to come off."

"Well, let's get to work on the rest of these, then," Marigold said. She hoped she'd know what to do, as she'd never scrubbed out a pot in her life.

Pretty soon Lazy Susan was giving her advice and correcting her technique, to the point where Marigold began to feel annoyed. Scrubbing pots wasn't dragon slaying, after all, and from what Marigold knew of Lazy Susan's reputation, she was certainly no expert on cleaning things.

"You must have been doing this for a long time," Marigold said, somewhat testily, pushing a strand of hair out of her eyes with the back of her hand.

"Not so long," Lazy Susan's voice echoed from inside a kettle. "I guess I must just have a knack for it."

Remembering what she was there for, Marigold decided it was time to get down to business. "I guess you must. But didn't I hear you'd been Queen Olympia's maid? How come you're in the scullery now?"

Lazy Susan backed out of the kettle. "Oooh, that—that—that *woman*," she said through clenched teeth, then proceeded to tell Marigold the whole story of how she and Angie had been friends, and what had happened after Angie turned into Olympia. "I couldn't believe how different she was then. Angie was sweet, and helpful, and had a sense of humor. Olympia is—" She stopped speaking abruptly, as if realizing that what she'd been about to say could be taken as treachery if said to the wrong person. Everyone in the castle had been very prudent in their conversations ever since they'd heard what happened to Swithbert, Ed, and Magnus.

"Why didn't you just go home?" Marigold asked her, really curious. "Back to Granolah." She was so stunned at the idea that for a year Olympia had been a nice person named Angie that she couldn't even think of a question to ask about that.

"I wanted—oh, you'll probably think this is silly— but I wanted to live in a castle for a while, just to see what it's like. My sister—my half sister, really—she's married to a prince, and she gets to live in one all the time."

"Living in a castle might not be what you expected."

"That's what Mrs. Clover says. And that's what I'm finding out. Now that you mention it, I might just about be ready to go home. Too bad this pretty castle isn't being run better."

"I know what you mean," Marigold said. "Sometimes I've wondered why everybody here doesn't just rise up and grab the queen and carry her down to the dungeon."

"Really?" Lazy Susan put down her scrub brush. "I've wondered that, too. I guess everybody's afraid of her. And there probably are some who would support her, and the riser-uppers would have to be afraid of them, too. If anyone even knew who they were."

"Do you think Rollo would be one of her supporters? With all his guards and archers? That would make a mutiny a lot harder, wouldn't it?"

"It's hard to tell about Rollo. His wife, Meg, is one of the kitchen maids and, to hear her talk, he's a big pussycat at home. Just a little jealous. But he loves being captain of the guards almost more than he loves Meg. Though she says sometimes he doesn't feel so good about doing things the queen orders him to do. But maybe he'd support anybody who'd let him still be captain."

"What if somebody sweetened that some?" Marigold said, thinking fast. "Gave him a fancier uniform, or a more important title, or a better horse?"

"From what I hear, I think he'd like that."

"What if I told you there was a plot forming to get rid of the queen? Would you be interested in joining in? If the answer is no, I'll deny I ever said any such thing to you."

Lazy Susan thought for a moment. Lying around in a hammock had once seemed like a pleasant way to spend her life, but she was starting to see that there was a lot of stuff going on in the world that she'd been missing out on completely. Some of the stuff was hard, and unpleasant, and even dangerous, but all of it was more interesting than lying in a hammock forever. And what could be more interesting (also dangerous and hard and, in parts, probably unpleasant) than a revolution? Might as well start in with her project of living a fuller life with the wildest possible thing.

"Sure," she said. "Count me in. If ever there was somebody just begging to be deposed, it's Olympia."

"Oh, great," Marigold said, clapping her hands. "Do you know anybody else we can count on for sure?"

"I haven't been here long enough to know very many people, but most of the kitchen staff seems pretty upset with Olympia, the way she wants special meals in the middle of the night, or orders a dish and then finds something wrong with it, and throws it on the floor. That's just rude."

"You're right," Marigold said, hoping she'd never done anything so impolite, or spoiled, or discourteous. Being royal could turn into a bad habit if you ever forgot, even for a minute, how fortunate you were. It was good to remember that a rebellion could be brewing at any time. It was good, too, to remember how hard a lot of people had to work to keep a kingdom running well, and that it was simply good manners to let them know, from time to time, how valued they were. "Well, do you think you could do a little inquiring—subtly, of course—in the next day or so and find out how much support there would be for a revolution? And I will, too."

"I'll do my best. But as long as we're stuck in here with these pots all day there isn't much we can do."

"Well, let's get these pots taken care of and get out of here," Marigold said, taking up a scrub brush and starting in with a vengeance on a particularly nasty accumulation of dragon fat. As she scrubbed, she thought about Olympia as a nice person named Angie and had trouble believing it could be possible.

# 26

Ed, Chris, Magnus, Swithbert, and Finbar spent a long, boring afternoon waiting for Marigold to return. They devised a game of throwing Ed's gold button at the little mice that scampered with regularity through the dungeon. But they were all lousy shots, and before long it seemed as if the mice were taunting them by sauntering saucily along the wall, or zigzagging brazenly across the floor. Still, they were glad they had Ed's salvaged button to relieve the tedium.

Ed was about ready to go after the little rascals with his bare hands when Marigold returned, carrying a kettle of gruel.

Proudly, she said, "I volunteered to do what nobody else likes to do: bring the prisoners their supper."

"I'm not sure we'll be thanking you, precious," Swithbert said.

Marigold set the kettle on the floor. "At least it's hot," she told them. "I insisted."

"Still not sure about any thanks," Chris said, examining the contents of the pot, though he was certainly thankful that she'd made it back without her true identity being discovered.

"I have to go back and get Finbar's supper. It's different from yours."

"Thank goodness," Finbar muttered.

"He's supposed to stay down here, on guard, until the trial," Marigold added.

"I thought for sure she'd have it today," Finbar said, "since it was Market Day, and there'd be such a big audience."

"Oh," Marigold said. "I found out she's so busy with fittings for a new wardrobe she didn't have time for a trial today. But it'll probably be on the next Market Day. She wanted to be sure she had the right outfit to wear to it."

"So we're stuck down here for another three days?" Swithbert asked.

"I'm not," Chris said. "I can go back to Zandelphia and smuggle in things that'll make your stay more comfortable."

"And I can bring things down from your quarters here," Marigold said. "As a maid, I'll have the run of the castle."

"You're going to keep being a maid for three more days?" Chris asked, aghast.

"Well, I sort of have to, don't I, if I'm going to try to organize a revolt from within. Which, by the way, seems to be a popular idea. It's even possible we could get Rollo to join us if we offer him some bonuses."

"She's right," Swithbert said. "She has to do it. It's the only way we can stay alert to the mood in the castle. But I have a hard time believing Rollo would join us. However, we shouldn't pass up anything that could give us an advantage."

"Could you please," Magnus put in diffidently, "bring me some clothes? At least some pants? I don't want to go on trial in my dressing gown."

"If everything goes the way we want it to," Marigold said, starting back up the stairs, "there won't be any trial. But I'll find you some pants anyway. Back in a bit with Finbar's dinner. Maybe I can also bring something from the kitchen to improve the gruel."

FOR THE NEXT couple of days, Marigold buzzed around the castle, staying out of Olympia's way and doing all she could to drum up support for the rebellion. It pleased her to know how fond the populace was of Swithbert, and how opposed most of them were to living under Olympia's ironfisted rule. But she was also dismayed to see how the emotional tide was turning against Swithbert because of his failure to control the queen. If Swithbert didn't take a stand, he would be deposed along with Olympia. Someone else the people liked better—maybe even Magnus, the king's closest direct relative not already ruling somewhere else—would inherit the kingdom of Beaurivage.

Marigold vowed she would remove her own liver with a rusty fork before she would scare her father with that news.

LAZY SUSAN, TOO, was spreading the word about a possible solution to the kingdom's discontent—and meeting a good many new people in the process. In Granolah she'd known everybody, and was so used to them that she barely paid them any attention anymore. Now, making so many new acquaintances made her feel all zippy with energy and curiosity—something she hadn't known could be so much fun.

She bumped into Mr. Lucasa on the stairs one afternoon. He was carrying a basket full of garments for Olympia, as well as a honey tart with a fancy crust that he'd made, and she was carrying a basket of beautiful fresh flowers from the gardens. Mrs. Clover had given her time off from the dirty pots as a reward for work well done, and she'd been assigned to distribute bouquets to the third-floor bedrooms. So hard work *did* have its rewards.

"Hello," she said. "I haven't seen you for days. What have you been doing?"

"Sewing, pinning, sewing some more, cooking, making cakes, trudging up and down stairs to run errands for an unreasonable woman, not getting much sleep. How about you?"

"Scrubbing, scrubbing, scrubbing, and also not getting very much sleep. Whoever said working in a castle was a good thing?"

"I'm not sure anybody ever said it," Mr. Lucasa said. "But most people need jobs, and the castle's where the jobs are."

"Would you say this castle is a good place to work?"

"I've never worked in any other so I can't really say, but all in all, I think I prefer working for myself. There is a lot of satisfaction in making things other people enjoy. But my primary customer here is somebody who's almost impossible to please, and there's not much satisfaction in that. There are times I want to call her a *Backpfeifengesicht.*"

"A *what*?"

"It's a German word. It means a face that cries out for a fist in it. But I'm keeping my temper under control. Anger hardly ever solves a problem, I've learned."

"But how about rebellion? Can't that sometimes solve a problem?"

"What do you mean? A rebellion against"—he lowered his voice—"the queen?"

She nodded a tiny nod.

"You just got here," he said, surprised. "And you're already involved in such a thing?"

"It doesn't take long to see how she operates. You already want to put your fist in her face. Think how people feel who've been working for her for a long time."

Mr. Lucasa rubbed his chin. He'd been so busy he hadn't had time to shave, and he'd begun growing a small white beard, which, Lazy Susan thought, was rather becoming on him. "You probably have a point. I've heard certain mutterings among the cooks and bakers. And I was told that Mrs. Vienna replaced a seamstress who got exiled because she'd left a pin in one of the queen's dresses and it poked her. The punishment seemed a bit drastic for the crime, in my opinion."

"All her punishments are drastic."

"So why don't you just go home?"

"I've thought about it," Lazy Susan said. "And I could. But now that I've seen how she reigns, I'd be wondering how the people I've met are doing, and it would keep me awake at night. I might as well stay and help them fix their situation. If I can. What about you?"

He was looking at her in a new way. Since he'd come to the castle, he'd heard about her reputation—her laziness, her jealousy of her half sister—but the person talking to him now was full of fire and animation. And if she was going to be involved in any kind of revolution, he wanted in on it, too.

"I know what you mean," he said. "And I don't want to leave, either, until I see if I can help. What should I do?"

"Just try to get more people involved. And let me know if you find anybody who's on the queen's side so we can figure out a way to neutralize them before the actual rebellion starts."

"Neutralize?" He didn't like the sound of that.

"I just mean get them out of the way. Lock them up someplace so they can't interfere. Or maybe change their minds. Afterward we can determine whether to exile them, or give them another chance, or whatever. I don't get to decide that. I'm not the one in charge here."

"Who is? Who's leading this rebellion?"

Lazy Susan scratched her head. "To tell you the truth, I don't actually know. I heard about it from another maid in the scullery. Her name's Mary—but I don't see how she could be the leader. She's just a scullery maid. And you should see how dirty she is!"

"I'd feel better if I knew who the leader is. We don't want to walk into a trap. Maybe the queen's trying to find out who in the castle opposes her in order to get rid of them. Maybe this Mary is a spy. We don't want to *kusat' sebe lokti.*"

"We don't want to *what?*"

"It's Russian for biting one's elbows. It's an expression that means sort of like crying over spilled milk. Carrying on over something you can't change. Regretting a mistake you can't correct. Like getting caught by the queen while planning a rebellion against her."

"Oh. Say, how many languages do you speak, anyway?"

"I've lost count. More than twelve, I'm pretty sure."

"Maybe you could teach me some words in other languages. It's handy to have a few, I can see that."

"With pleasure. Now I've got to get these things

up to the queen before she says I can't have any supper for three days. And as you can see, I like my supper." He rubbed his little potbelly.

LATER, IN THE SCULLERY, Lazy Susan mentioned to Marigold that the plans for the rebellion might be a trick by Olympia to ferret out any more traitors.

"Oh, no," Marigold said. "I know that's not true. I know where the idea came from."

"You do? Who?"

"I can't say. It's a secret. The fewer people who know, the safer. I wouldn't want anything happening to you because you know. You know?"

"But I wouldn't tell anybody."

"You don't know what you'd do under torture," Marigold said darkly. "Nobody does."

"Oh," Lazy Susan said. "Torture."

"I'm sorry. But I must protect you. You'll thank me someday."

"I hope so. I'm getting nervous. I was up on the third floor this afternoon arranging flowers when Mr. Lucasa, the queen's new chef and couturier, brought her some outfits, and I could hear her yelling all the way from her quarters about something she didn't like. And it wasn't even anything important. Just a bow in the wrong place, or something."

"Her and her darn bows," Marigold muttered.

"What?"

"Oh, it's just those bows. She's got to have a bow on everything! And she wants everybody else to have bows on everything, too."

"Sounds like you know her pretty well."

"Uh, well, I've been around for a long time. And it's . . . it's hard to ignore so many bows. As for the yelling, she's good at that, too."

"It'll be nice, then, when it's over. If this thing works."

"Right."

Marigold was getting nervous, too. So far, things had been going so smoothly that she was beginning to think something was wrong. Nothing went *that* smoothly. No one but Finbar was checking on the dungeon, no one seemed to notice the new maid in the scullery, none of the many subjects of the kingdom who now knew about the impending revolt had leaked any information to anyone who shouldn't know about it, and nobody had heard a single word about whether a trial actually would be occurring on the next Market Day.

Naturally things couldn't stay this uncomplicated.

# 27

The first complication was this: Olympia sent a couple of new guards down to check on Finbar. Relieving him would be something that wouldn't occur to her. But checking up on people—that was something she was experienced at.

The guards, Somerset and Grumley, arrived while Finbar, Swithbert, and Magnus (gratefully wearing a smuggled-in pair of pants and a shirt under his dressing gown) were napping. Marigold was out and about in the castle, and Chris had gone out the disposal tunnel to look in on affairs in Zandelphia. Ed, grown bold by days with no one actively guarding them, had left Finbar (who had taken to sleeping in Ed's cell, the biggest one) and crept out to rummage in the tumbled heap of his possessions piled at the farthest, darkest end of the dungeon.

When he heard Somerset and Grumley clomping down the stairs, he froze, hidden in the dark, up to his hips in his precious collections.

"Finbar!" Grumley shouted, waking not only Finbar, but Swithbert and Magnus as well. "What's happened here? Why are you in there? Why are the cell doors open? Where's the other prisoner?"

Finbar jerked upright, pillow creases on his cheek. "Huh?" he said.

"And where did you get a pillow?" Somerset shouted. "Cells aren't supposed to have pillows."

Finbar staggered to his feet. "Pillow?" he said stupidly, stalling for time. "Why, it must have been left behind when the cells were cleaned out." He knew perfectly well it was one of the ones Marigold had brought from the castle linen cupboard.

"I don't think so," Grumley said in a menacing tone. He had known Finbar since they were boys, and knew what a perfectly dreadful liar he was. "What's going on down here?" He put his hand on the sword strapped to his hip.

Ed, perched in his pile of junk, furtively felt around for something he could use as a weapon, but there seemed to be nothing but scarves and socks and knit caps.

By this time Magnus and Swithbert were awake and quaking on their cots, afraid to move.

"You wouldn't be fixing to help these prisoners escape, would you?" Somerset asked.

"Do I look crazy?" Finbar felt pretty crazy just then. "The queen would have me stretched on the rack for that. I admit, I wouldn't mind being a little taller, but I don't want to add a few inches *that* badly."

"Then what *are* you doing?" Grumley asked.

"I'm, uh, I was, uh . . ." Finbar's natural instinct was to tell the truth, and his attempts to override that were always obvious, even to someone who wasn't paying much attention. And sometimes, like just then, he couldn't do it at all. "Say. You fellows wouldn't be interested in seeing King Swithbert back on the throne, would you?" he blurted.

Ed gasped so loudly he was sure they would hear him. But *his* gasps were drowned out by Magnus's and Swithbert's.

"Back on the throne?" Somerset asked. "With Queen Olympia, you mean? How's that going to happen when he's about to be tried for treason?"

"Don't, Finbar," Swithbert said, while Magnus made little gurgling sounds and Ed kept hyperventilating.

Finbar looked over at Swithbert, shrugged, and kept going. "I mean by himself. Sole ruler."

Somerset scratched his head with the dirk he was holding. "I don't get it."

"Think about it," Finbar said. "Are you having a good time working for the queen?"

"Well, all us guards have been a lot busier. And a lot nervouser, since she's always upset about something. And she wants us to be a lot meaner, which not all of us like. I myself prefer to think that I'm serving as the people's protector, not the people's punisher."

"Hey, you're right," Grumley said, letting go of his sword hilt. "Heroic in battle is one thing. Picking on unarmed people is something else. But what's that got to do with the king and treason?"

"Well, let's say he's innocent. Let's say the queen just wants him out of the way so she can take over the kingdom without any interference now that she's changed the constitution so it says she can succeed him. Let's say she lives to be a *very* old lady, getting crankier and more demanding with each passing year, turning the kingdom into a place that exists just to satisfy her whims and pleasures. Does that sound like a good thing?"

Somerset scratched his head some more with the dirk, and Grumley rubbed his jaw thoughtfully.

Ed didn't think it was that hard a question, but he kept himself from blurting out the answer by stuffing a sock in his mouth.

Finally, Grumley said, "Not to me."

"Me, either," Somerset said.

"Okay, then." Finbar cheerfully clapped his hands together. "We've got to get the king back on the throne, don't we? That means we need to get the queen off."

"But isn't that—treason?" Somerset asked. "Isn't that why Swithbert's in here?"

"If you're on the right side, it's called a people's revolution," Finbar said. "And you're a man of the people, right?"

Swithbert had long since shut up and let Finbar go. He was so persuasive he could have a new career as some kind of salesman or minister instead of a guard. Swithbert made a note to himself to put those talents to work if he ever got Beaurivage back.

"Uh, I guess so," Somerset said.

Grumley nodded. "Does that mean we're part of the plot now?"

"It's not a plot," Finbar said. "It's an act of liberation. How many of the other guards do you think feel the way you do?"

"I'd say . . . most of them," Somerset said. "There's

a few who think the queen is the greatest, but they're the ones I'm a little scared of myself. And there's a couple who think anybody who has a ferret has got to be okay, just because they're big ferret fans. But they could probably be convinced. When's this happening? It better be soon because the queen's setting up a gallows in the bailey. And Market Day is tomorrow. You know how she likes a big audience."

Swithbert finally had something to say. "So I guess we know when the trial's going to be and how it's going to turn out."

"Was there any doubt how it would turn out?" Grumley asked.

"I suppose not," Swithbert admitted.

"So, here's your job," Finbar went on. "Find out how many of the guards we can count on. And crazy as it may sound, don't forget Rollo. Come back and tell me, and we can go from there. Oh—and it should go without saying, stay out of the way of the queen."

After Grumley and Somerset had gone back upstairs, Swithbert came out of his cell and shook Finbar's hand with both his own. "I thought for sure we were goners right there on the spot, but you were brilliant. When this is over, you're getting a big promotion." He paused. "Only if we win, of course."

"Of course," Finbar agreed.

Ed emerged from the shadows, removing the sock from his mouth and saying, "I don't want to be putting the cat before the horse, but there may be some stuff in that pile that we can use."

At that same moment, Marigold came padding down the stairs, and Chris came crawling in through the disposal tunnel, and they had to be brought up to date. Marigold had brought some treacle tarts, which they ate while they worked on their strategy.

"These are the best treacle tarts I've ever tasted," Swithbert said. "Surely the same cook who used to make those runny eggs didn't make these."

"There's a new chef," Marigold told him. "He came with Olympia and Lazy Susan. He's fixing some of her dresses, too. Seems like he can do about anything. Lazy Susan says he's the most creative person she's ever seen. And he can put up with Olympia better than most, too, even though he doesn't really care for her tactics."

"He sounds too good to be real," Swithbert said. "I can't wait to meet him. I hope I get the chance."

"Me, too."

And then they went back to their planning. The next day they would find out if their plans would work, and no one was sure. Olympia wasn't an easy person to fool, and she would be especially vigilant about pulling off such an important act before a big crowd. She would have to make dear old Swithbert look wicked and dangerous, and then execute him, along with Ed and Magnus, in public. And she'd have to do it with such confidence and authority that no one in the castle, or the crowd, would consider questioning her actions or interfering with her.

None of them doubted for a moment that she was perfectly capable of all that.

NOR DID SHE. At that very moment she was standing in front of her full-length mirror, wearing the execution-day gown Mr. Lucasa had sewn for her, practicing her royal wave. And then her royal signal to the executioner to pull the nooses tight.

# 28

The next complication was that Mrs. Clover noticed Marigold.

Maybe Marigold had taken too many chances running around the castle she knew by heart, forgetting that she was supposed to be a simple maid. She'd thought she was being careful, but ordinary maids didn't help themselves to a pan of cooling treacle tarts, or get glimpsed carrying a pile of feather pillows with the imperial crest on them down the dungeon stairs, or keep very irregular working hours. Or stay so dirty.

Somebody as attentive as Mrs. Clover wasn't going to miss things like that for very long. She stopped Marigold outside the pantry when Marigold, thinking too hard about what was to happen the next day, walked out with a bowl of hoofenpoofer goulash for her father.

"Where do you think you're taking that, young lady?" Mrs. Clover asked. "I'm not aware that anyone has ordered a bowl of hoofenpoofer goulash. And you better not be eating it yourself. You know servants eat only at assigned times." She peered more closely at Marigold, who ducked her head and let her hair fall over her face. "You look familiar to me, but I can't put a name to you. And I don't remember hiring you. How long have you worked here?"

Marigold, unlike Finbar, was a pretty good liar. She'd had a lot of practice growing up, trying to keep things from Olympia. But then, she'd had time to prepare her lies in advance. Now she'd been taken by surprise, and caught red-handed as well.

"Uh, my name's Mary. I, uh, I ain't been here too long. I can't say 'zactly when I came." She quickly decided her best defense was to keep her head down and to appear as foolish as possible. In her experience, people gave up too fast with those they believed to be stupid. Patience might be a virtue, but in Marigold's view it wasn't practiced often enough.

"Well, I would have been the one who interviewed you, and I don't have any recollection of that. And I certainly would have remembered someone as dirty as you are. And as out of uniform. And as hangdog. I don't permit any of the castle's workers to go around looking as you do. It's a disgrace. And Beaurivage has a reputation to uphold. I believe you've sneaked in here thinking you could get free food and lodging by pretending to be employed here. It happens from time to time. But no one goes undiscovered for long."

Marigold quickly decided further lying or arguing would get her nowhere. She'd known Mrs. Clover all her life, after all, and knew she was not a lady to be messed with. That was why she hadn't dared mention the rebellion to her, even though she might have been sympathetic. So Marigold hung her head even lower and murmured, "Uh-huh."

"Just as I thought," Mrs. Clover said. "I'll have Rollo escort you out across the drawbridge. Come with me. Oh—and give me that bowl of hoofenpoofer goulash. You've had your last meal courtesy of Beaurivage Castle."

Marigold certainly hoped that wasn't true. She allowed herself to be pulled along, keeping her head down in what was meant to look like shame.

She kept her face averted while Rollo took great pleasure in marching her to the end of the drawbridge with his sword point in her back. Once she'd stepped into the dirt of the road that led away from the castle, he shouted, "I'll be watching for you, so don't try sneaking in here again! Next time you'd go before the queen, and I know you wouldn't like that."

Rollo definitely had that right, Marigold thought. "I've heard about your queen," she shot back. "Sounds to me like she's just asking for an uprising."

Rollo blinked. "How long were you in the castle?" he asked.

"Dunno. Few days." She shaded her eyes with her hand to shield her face. "Why?"

"And in that short a time you heard about an uprising?"

"Didn't hear about one. Just heard how miserable and browbeaten and suspicious a lot of the subjects and the workers are. The queen should know better. *Anybody* should know better than to do what she's doing. Just makes people mad. And sooner'd you want to guess, they're going to do something about it." She paused. "Don't you think?" Here was her chance to see if what Lazy Susan had suggested could be true. But she had to be very careful not to give anything away in case it wasn't.

Rollo was quiet for some time—and he *did* appear to be thinking. Finally he said, "You could be right."

"I *am* right," Marigold said. "I've been thinking

about it longer than you have." And she had. From childhood she'd watched her parents rule and thought about what she would do differently if she ever got the chance. In one of the first in-person conversations she'd had with Christian, they'd talked about how they would run kingdoms, which was strange since at that time, neither of them thought they'd ever do such a thing.

"Yeah." Rollo seemed to be talking to himself. "I think you are."

Marigold was about to offer him some inducements, unlikely as it was that he would believe she had the power to grant them, when he said in a louder voice, "Go on now. Go back to where you came from. And don't think you can get in the castle again without me catching you."

She had missed her chance! She had no choice but to turn away and begin walking down the dirt road toward the Zandelphia-Beaurivage Bridge. As she walked, she wondered what his agreement meant. Was he actually thinking of participating in a revolt? Or of tipping Olympia off that there was a possibility that one could be on the way?

As for not being able to sneak back into the castle—well, ha! She could be back inside via the disposal tunnel within half an hour.

And she was.

"You have to go back," Finbar said after she'd told them what had happened. "You have to go back and tell him what he can have if he joins the rebellion."

"Me?" Marigold said. "I'd never get close enough to Rollo now to tell him anything. I can't go back into the castle from here. Mrs. Clover would spot me right away. And I can't get in across the drawbridge. Why would Rollo believe me even if I *could* get to him? I'm just a dirty castle-crasher as far as he's concerned. He's under orders not to let me in as myself, either, so forget it."

"I'll tell him," Chris said. "He'd have to believe me. I've got credentials *and* clout."

"And he's under orders not to let *you* in, too," Marigold reminded him.

"Oh, yeah. Well, *somebody's* got to make him an offer he can't refuse."

They all looked at one another, weighing the reasons why none of them could do it, even as they recognized that with Rollo on their side, the odds of Ed, Swithbert, and Magnus avoiding becoming history, as well as toast, were greatly increased.

"I still have the livery I wore when I was a servant here," Christian said. "I kept it as a souvenir. I can go get it and wear it to approach Rollo. I'll wear a false mustache so nobody recognizes me."

Marigold's heart almost stopped at the thought of the serious risks Chris would take in such an operation. She wanted to tell him he couldn't do it, that she couldn't bear to have anything happen to him. But then she remembered that she was a queen. And queens—good ones, anyway—had to put the good of the people they were responsible for ahead of their own personal desires. Maybe not just queens should do that, she thought. Maybe everybody should. But since she *was* a queen, she really had no choice. And because Christian was a king, he didn't, either.

She took a deep breath, blinked back her tears, and said, "That's the only plan that makes sense. And we're running out of time. You'd better hurry."

With that, Chris gave her a quick hug, rushed into the disposal tunnel, and disappeared.

The time before he returned was filled with pacing, hand-wringing, worrying, and feeble attempts from each of them to cheer up the others. *Feeble* being the operative word: the attempts were completely unsuccessful.

Chris returned with a bundle holding the livery, the fake mustache, and also a shaggy gray wig left over from a costume party he and Marigold had thrown to celebrate their first anniversary. Once he was dressed, he looked so ridiculous that it was hard to imagine Rollo would even be able to talk to him without laughing. But in disguise was the only way for him to go into the castle, so he kissed Marigold, shook hands with Finbar, Ed, Swithbert, and Magnus, and started up the stairs.

# 29

Christian tiptoed along corridors, ducking behind drapes or statuary whenever he heard anyone coming. As he ran through the deserted Hall of Mirrors, he caught a million quick glimpses of himself and hoped that he didn't really look as demented as the blurry, fractured images suggested.

Gradually Chris made his way to the guardsmen's quarters and loitered outside their ready room, crouching behind a large leather chest with assorted weapons spilling from it. If Rollo took offense to anything he had to say, there would certainly be no shortage of items with which to be run through. Chris shuddered, then braced himself. This was no time to get cold feet. He had a mission. A lot of people would benefit from what he had to do. If he did it right.

He hid behind the chest for quite a while, through one changing of the guard (accompanied by a lot of weapon-clattering), a long, boring conversation about the merits of different kinds of chain mail, and finally silence as all the off-duty guards went to dinner. And Rollo never put in an appearance.

Just when Chris thought he would have to go out into the castle again to hunt Rollo down, he heard footsteps and, peeking out from behind the chest, saw him coming along the corridor alone. At eight feet tall, Rollo was always an impressive figure, but at that moment, he was not at his finest. His eyes were cast down, his shoulders slumped, and he was dragging his sword along so carelessly that Christian could see (with relief) that the tip was being dulled and bent.

Chris waited until Rollo had gone into the ready room before he came out from behind the chest and tiptoed into the room, too. Rollo was sitting in a chair, his back to the door, untying his cuirass. His sword lay on the table beside him.

Chris closed the door and cleared his throat. Rollo grabbed his sword, jumped to his feet, and whirled around. When he saw Chris, dressed in Beaurivage livery, he lowered his blade, gave a choked laugh, and said, "What in the devil do you want? And who's your barber?"

Chris felt his wig, relieved that Rollo didn't seem to recognize him. "Does it look that bad?"

"It's pathetic, man," Rollo said. "Looks like it's been gnawed by a ferret. Better not let Sedgewick see you or he'll have your head shaved. Which, come to think of it, would be a big improvement. Did you want something?"

Chris nodded. "I need to speak to you in confidence."

Rollo spread his long arms. "Nobody in here but us. Go ahead."

Chris cleared his throat and shot a quick look back, calculating how fast he could get the door open if he had to run for his life. "I'm here to make you an offer. A very good offer."

Rollo laughed, loudly this time. "*You*? What have *you* got to offer *me*?"

Chris stood very straight and resisted trying to smooth his wig. "I'm authorized to offer you a new title—major-general of the guards—as well as a new uniform, a better steed, and a medal."

Rollo squinted at him. "Say again?"

So Chris said it again.

"Authorized by who?" Rollo asked.

"By the king of Beaurivage, and the king and queen of Zandelphia."

"Huh," Rollo grunted, and scratched his head. "And why would those folks want to do all that for me?" he asked suspiciously. "By the way, in case you haven't heard, the king of Beaurivage is being tried for treason tomorrow morning, so he might not actually have too much to say about what happens around here."

"That's why he wants to give you these things. So you'll help him"—Christian had to stop for a breath before he plunged into dangerous territory—"with his rebellion."

"Rebellion?" Rollo boomed. "There's going to be a rebellion?"

Chris resisted the impulse to put his finger to his lips. "That's the plan. I mean, the hope."

"Who are you, anyway? What's some footman with a rotten haircut, who I'm pretty sure I've never seen before, doing with an offer like that? You wouldn't be a spy from Queen Olympia, would you, trying to test my loyalty? Trying to get me put on trial tomorrow, too? Because, if you are, you should know I wouldn't take very kindly to that." He raised his sword and ran his thumb along the edge of it, stopping with a puzzled look when he got to the bent tip.

*This is the moment,* Chris thought, and whipped off his wig. "Now do you know me?"

Rollo leaned forward and squinted. "King Christian? Of Zandelphia? Really?" His mouth made a big O.

"That's me."

"How—how did you get in here? All my guards know the queen has forbidden your entrance into the castle. Who let you in? The queen will have his head."

"Nobody *let* me in. I have my own ways of access. That's beside the point. Which is that there's a revolt on the way. The people of Beaurivage deserve better ruling than they're getting from Olympia. Swithbert should be back on the throne. We have reason to believe that a good number of the citizenry will be with us, and also most of your guards. But we know it will go faster and smoother, and with less—uh—mayhem—if you're in it, too. And if you are, there'll be the title, the uniform, etc. If not—well, you'll take your chances."

"You're serious?"

"Never more."

"You're really going to rebel against the queen?"

"Didn't I just say that?" Chris was getting exasperated. He wanted a yes or a no—and right now. Not all this dancing around. They were running out of time. If Rollo said no, the rebellion would have to start instantly.

"What happens if you lose?" Rollo asked.

"Probably nothing good, wouldn't you think?"

"Yeah, that's what I'd think."

They stood there looking at each other. Chris observed that Rollo hadn't turned loose of his sword, though he hadn't raised it, either, so there was no clear indication of his intentions.

*One more try,* Chris thought. "The queen has been very unkind to many people. King Swithbert has never been anything but benevolent. Which style of leadership do you think your fellow Beaurivageans would thank you for helping them achieve?"

"Some admire how Olympia rules."

"True, I suppose. Is that your answer?"

He sighed. "No. But when you're eight feet tall and captain of the guards, people expect a certain degree of heartlessness and inhumanity."

"Maybe you could show them that being eight feet tall and rigorous in the pursuit of justice for everybody is better than being eight feet tall and heartless. You don't want to be a stereotype, do you?"

Rollo sighed again. "You don't have to bribe me with the title and the uniform and all that. I'm tired of heartlessness and cruelty. It wears on you after a while, you know. Especially when you're thinking about becoming a father. I'll help. I want to."

"Good man. You won't be sorry." *I hope,* Chris thought. "And good luck with the father project. I'm thinking about it myself."

"Just tell me what you want me to do."

Rollo didn't sound very happy, but Chris hoped that was because he was scared and worried about the outcome, not because he wasn't convinced. *Well, join the club,* he thought.

After a long explanation of the plan to Rollo, Chris said, "You can't change your mind now."

"I won't. Just don't wear that wig tomorrow, okay?"

"You've got a deal. Now I've got to go. But I'll see you tomorrow."

FAR ABOVE THEIR HEADS, in Olympia's suite, she also was looking ahead to the next day. But she was doing it with glee.

# 30

Lazy Susan asked Mr. Lucasa how many people he reckoned were in favor of the rebellion.

"Everyone I've talked to," he said. "With odds like that it seems the problem should be able to be solved by *ho'oponopono*. But knowing the queen, I see that it's not possible."

"*Ho'oponopono?*"

"It's Hawaiian. It means solving a problem by talking it out."

"With Olympia? Pardon me while I say 'ha'!"

"Precisely. Do you know when it's to be?"

"Tomorrow. What we're supposed to do is gather up everybody who is on our side, pass out all the weapons from Ed's collections left behind in the dungeon, and be ready when King Christian from Zandelphia springs the trap. It's going to be during the trial of King Swithbert and the others. We're supposed to pass the word along."

"You've gone to a lot of trouble to help with this. I'm somewhat surprised. I'd heard that you, well, that you were rather *haochi-lanzuo*."

She just looked at him.

"Oh. Well, it's Chinese. It means to be fond of food, but averse to work."

She looked down at her shoes. In Granolah, where everyone accepted her as she was, being *haochi-lanzuo* had seemed perfectly reasonable. But since she'd been in Beaurivage and had seen how necessary real work was to keep a society functioning, and how important it was for workers to cooperate and help each other, she had begun to feel differently about her slothful existence. Too, she'd experienced the satisfaction of a job well done—even one that involved dragon fat and hoofenpoofer juice.

Meekly, she said, "I must confess, that used to be true. But I don't think it is anymore. And as far as the rebellion—I like feeling a part of something big and important, knowing it could benefit a lot of people."

"And what if the revolt fails?" Mr. Lucasa asked. "What if it turns out to be a *yabu hebi ni naru*?" He added, "It's Japanese for something that backfires. Literally, it means to poke at a bush and get a snake."

"A nice way to refer to the queen," Susan said drily. "But accurate. Well, if it fails, we'll be taking the consequences—and I'm sure they won't be pretty. But the effort is necessary. I really think so. And once you see something that needs to be done, it just makes you feel all itchy and uncomfortable until you take care of it. Doesn't it?"

Mr. Lucasa smiled. "Congratulations. You've met your conscience. In my experience, the world is divided between those who have one and those who don't. And the ones with one are divided into those who will act on their conscience and those who won't. Those who will are, I'm afraid, the smallest category. They will *jeito*. It's Brazilian Portuguese. It means to find a way to get something done, no matter what the obstacles."

"Well, I guess I'm going to *jeito*. At least for tomorrow."

OF COURSE, NOBODY who knew what the next day would be bringing slept a wink that night.

Ed spent the long hours muttering imprecations

at the guards who had made such a mess of his collections as they dug through them, searching for usable weapons.

Finbar, Magnus, and Swithbert played snipsnapsnorum with a deck of cards Ed had unearthed until Finbar owed the king more money than he would ever see in a lifetime—at which time he outright accused the king of cheating.

"Well, of course I cheat," Swithbert said, unfazed. "Everybody knows that. That's why nobody but Ed will play with me anymore. He cheats, too, so it's even. I thought you knew that. Magnus, you knew that, right?"

Magnus nodded. "But playing keeps my mind off what could go wrong tomorrow. Now that you mention it, though, in what might be my last hours I should be doing something more—I don't know—more noble, or more significant."

"Don't talk like that," Marigold interjected. She was scared and worried and having palpitations already, and didn't want anybody making it worse. "I know. I'll teach you a new kind of joke I learned. It takes two people so, Magnus, I'll start with you. Knock, knock."

"What?"

"Not *what*," she said. "You have to say 'who's there?'"

"Oh. Who's there, then?"

"Boo."

"Are you trying to scare me?" He looked to Swithbert for help, but the king just shrugged. "I'm already scared."

"No!" Marigold said, exasperated. "You have to ask 'who?'"

"I don't get this," Magnus said. "And I don't think it's very funny, either. It's not helping me be less nervous."

"Wait. Let me demonstrate with Christian." Which she did, and when they got to the punch lines (Boo who? I'm sorry I made you cry.), everyone understood how it worked, but talking about crying didn't make anybody feel any better.

"I think I'll write Sephronia a letter," Magnus said, "just in case I don't get another chance to explain things to her. Though I'm not sure I really *can* explain what went wrong the last time I saw her."

"When was that?" Christian asked.

Magnus remembered all too well. "It was right after Queen Olympia came back to Beaurivage."

Christian looked over at Marigold and nodded. "You were right," he told her. "She did release something noxious into the air." Turning back to Magnus, he said, "We were all breathing in some of Olympia's bad effusions, and it made us behave in strange ways. I think even the dogs were affected. It explains all that growling and fighting they've been doing."

"We were breathing Olympia's effusions?" Magnus asked. "Well, *yuck!* And how am I going to explain *that* to Sephronia?" He sighed. "Ed, can you find any ink and paper in that pile? I guess I'd better at least try."

"Does anybody want to do another knock-knock joke?" Marigold asked. "This one will be better, I promise."

Swithbert, always the good father, said (after a silence that went on a bit too long), "Certainly, precious. Knock, knock."

"Who's there?" Marigold asked.

He scratched his head. "I have no idea. Am I doing something wrong?"

"Oh! I'm the one who's supposed to say 'knock, knock.' The person who knows how the joke comes out says it. So, Papa, knock, knock."

"Who is it?"

Marigold stopped herself from correcting him, and said, "Archie."

Swithbert looked over at Christian, who whispered, "Archie who?"

"Oh," Swithbert said. "Archie who?"

"Gesundheit!" Marigold exclaimed, and clapped her hands.

"I didn't sneeze," Swithbert said.

"I know, I know. But when you said 'Archie who?' it sounds enough like a sneeze so that when I said 'Gesundheit,' the joke makes sense. Oh, I just love knock-knock jokes! Ed, give me some of that paper and ink. I want to make up a few more."

While Marigold was busy with her joke writing, Swithbert turned to Christian and murmured, "These knock-knock jokes will never catch on. They're way too complicated, and not very funny."

"I couldn't agree more," Chris murmured back. "I don't know what Wendell was thinking when he taught them to Marigold."

"Wendell the wizard?" Swithbert interrupted. "What's he got to do with all this?"

"He's over at the cave-castle in Zandelphia. Marigold called him in to help us do something about Olympia."

"Wendell? He's the last person I'd call in for something important."

"Actually, he *was* the last person. Which is why I didn't want to tell you that he's going to be part of the revolution."

"Oh, good grief," Swithbert said. "*Now* you tell me. I hope he's not a very big part."

"Hmmm," Chris said. "How about another hand of snipsnapsnorum? Don't worry, I know you cheat."

OLYMPIA WAS playing cards, too, just then. With her favorite partner: herself. She had laid out a hand of solitaire and was moving the cards to create a better arrangement. She hadn't a care in the world. Everything was planned to a tee for execution day—and then she would be queen all by herself, without Swithbert in the way.

She scratched Fenleigh's neck and said, "How would you like a little crown, Fenleigh? You can be my consort." And then she laughed uproariously at her own wit.

# 31

After a long, long night, morning finally came. Ed had fallen asleep on his pile of possessions, and the others had continued with the joke writing, letter writing, and cheating at cards until they, too, had dozed off where they sat. Not even terror and trepidation can keep exhausted people awake. Sleep is the escape hatch for overburdened minds.

Finbar was the first to awaken, the result of years of military discipline. When he saw his fellow conspirators sprawled out around him, snoring and drooling, he had a moment of great dread. The revolution depended on *these* people? They didn't look capable of organizing a bake sale.

Before he could lose his nerve and run upstairs, ready to blab the whole plan to the queen, he forced himself to remember how much he didn't want to live under her boot. Even if the plan didn't work, he had to know that he had tried.

He straightened his uniform, licked his palms and smoothed his hair with them, and woke King Swithbert first. "It's time, sire," he said. "Today's the day of your execution."

This announcement is guaranteed to get a sleeping person on his feet instantly. Which it did.

"I hope never again in my lifetime to hear those words," Swithbert said as he rubbed the sleep from his eyes.

Soon everyone was awake and surprisingly hungry. They had all assumed apprehension would kill their appetites, but instead it seemed to have made them hungrier. No one wanted to utter the words "last meal," but perhaps that's what they were all thinking. Because they hadn't expected to be so hungry, they had not asked Christian to bring in adequate breakfast provisions from Zandelphia.

They shared what unsatisfying leftovers they had, hoping it would be enough to see them through what lay ahead. "There's not even any gruel," Ed said. "I'm sure Olympia doesn't want to waste any provisions on the condemned."

"I'd prefer it if you didn't refer to us as the condemned," Magnus said. "We haven't been tried yet." He pulled his dressing gown closer. Even though he now had on a shirt and pants, he'd grown attached to the garment he'd been wearing for days on end. Besides, it seemed appropriate to keep it on as long as he was still wearing his bedroom slippers.

Swithbert gave him a baleful look, indicating he had no faith in the fairness of Olympia's trials, even if they were to get one.

"I think we'll be more alert if we're a bit on the hungry side," Marigold said brightly. "It'll give us an excuse for a big celebratory meal once we've taken care of our business."

This announcement was met with sullen silence. But there was nothing they could do except sit listening to their growling stomachs and glaring at Christian as he started out the disposal tunnel to prepare for his part in the rebellion.

He noticed the glares and came back. "I promise I won't eat a bite while I'm over in Zandelphia getting ready. My middle name is Solidarity."

"It is?" Finbar asked. "Funny name."

"It's not really Solidarity," Christian explained patiently. "I was just indicating supportiveness. Actually, I have three middle names. Errol Achilles Linus."

"That's nothing," Ed said. "My whole name is Edric Ulf Orion. Orion means 'giant' in Latin. Great name for a guy who's four feet tall, don't you think? My parents *knew* I was a troll. What were they thinking? Anyway, that's the whole name I want on my headstone."

"There aren't going to be any headstones," Chris said. "I'm pretty sure. Now I've got to get going, but I'll see you soon at the trial." He kissed Marigold thoroughly and then disappeared out the disposal tunnel.

He hadn't been gone more than a few minutes when the sound of many marching feet could be heard coming down the stone steps. Magnus, Ed, and Swithbert quickly went into their cells, where Finbar locked them in. Marigold hid in the shadows behind Ed's pile of discarded treasures, and Finbar stood at attention, waiting.

A unit of guards, with Rollo at its head, came pounding down the stairs and stood in formation in the corridor between the rows of cells. "At ease," Rollo said, and the guards supposedly relaxed, but not in any way that was apparent to the naked eye.

Finbar raised his pike in salute. He'd been informed by Christian that Rollo was on their side, but in a castle as full of intrigue as this one was, he wasn't taking any chances. Not until he had to, anyway.

Rollo came close to Finbar and, looming above him, said, "So what happens now?"

"Well, uh, now we take the prisoners up to the queen for trial, don't we?" he said cautiously.

Rollo gave Finbar a hard look. "I know *that*. I mean, how soon before the"—he lowered his voice, but it still echoed all through the dungeon—"rebellion begins?"

"Didn't King Christian tell you?"

"Yes. But I'm the edgy type. Tell me again."

"Well, he'll be coming with a surprise. We have to be up in the bailey with as many armed rebels as we can gather, ready when he blows the whistle. Then we surround the queen and hold off any of her defenders. Since it's Market Day, there'll be a lot of peasants and farmers there who haven't heard what's going on, so we'll have to watch out for them. You never know—some of them might want to support the queen, and they could give us trouble."

Out of the shadows came Marigold, filthy and

ragged and completely unconvincing as a queen. "But I'm sure there are enough of us from the castle to keep things under control. I'd prefer to avoid any bloodshed. People with weapons threatening those without them usually works just fine as a means of restraint."

"Who's that?" Rollo asked Finbar.

"Why, that's Queen Marigold."

"It is not," Rollo said. "It's true she wasn't a very good dresser when she lived here, but she never looked *that* bad. I think that's the interloper Mrs. Clover had me kick out of the castle yesterday."

Marigold giggled. "This is a disguise, Rollo. I've been able to go all over the castle like this."

"Excuse me, then, Your Majesty," he said, still eyeing her dubiously. "It's a better disguise than that awful wig your husband was wearing, I'll say that. But shouldn't you be more dressed up so you can have some authority when you go out against Olympia? She sets great store by outfits, you know."

"I do know. I haven't forgotten all those awful gowns she made me wear when I was growing up. Now I like to think my authority comes from the way I comport myself—as well as the *moral* authority of my cause."

Rollo still looked dubious, but he'd been well trained to not argue with queens. "I guess I'd better round up the prisoners, then, and take them up for their trial. And don't worry—all these guards know what's going on, and they can be trusted."

At that, Somerset and Grumley wiggled their fingers in a little wave, and then stood back at attention.

Rollo went on. "Another guard will be down in a few minutes to get the rest of Ed's weapons and distribute them to those rebels who are still unarmed. All right, let's go."

Finbar unlocked the cell doors, and Ed, Magnus, and Swithbert came out. Rollo bound their hands behind them and led them up the stairs, with Finbar taking up the rear. Even when one knows the guards are on your side, and that a rebellion is on the way, a hungry person in bondage can be excused for having a heavy sinking feeling at the thought that everything might not work out exactly as planned.

Swithbert cast an anxious glance back at Marigold before he vanished around the curve in the staircase, leaving her alone in the dungeon. She was experiencing a bit of her own sinking feeling just then.

After the sound of footsteps faded, she stood, still

looking up the empty staircase, wondering if their plan could possibly work.

Then she gave herself a hard shake and thought maybe Rollo was right about the way she looked. She should at least wash her face and hands before she went up against her so-called mother.

# 32

Olympia sat on the throne that had until recently been Swithbert's, which had been carried out into the castle courtyard by a few grudging servants who hoped that was the last command of hers they'd ever have to obey. The throne was put up onto a platform, from which Olympia waved regally to her subjects, some of whom had come in from the countryside to find their Market Day decorated with three gallows, three hangmen dressed in black (including masks), and a queen so done up in jewels, medals, and brooches that the glare was positively blinding. Not to mention the ferret on her shoulder, which wore a jeweled collar.

As those subjects gaped and others waited tensely, the troop of guards escorting Ed, Magnus, and Swithbert came marching into the bailey, scattering the gapers who then had even more to gape at.

The prisoners were lined up in front of the queen, who looked down at them with a smile. "Hungry?" she asked, speaking so softly that only they could hear.

Of course there was no answer. Anyway, she could hear their stomachs growling.

"I decided not to waste any final gruel on you," she said, "since you weren't going to be around long enough to digest it."

"We could be found innocent," Swithbert said. "That's what a fair trial implies."

Olympia waved her hand dismissively. "Of course a trial is important. But a trial is just a formality if the culprits are clearly guilty. As you three are."

"You still need proof. Or else it's just your opinion," Swithbert argued. He knew it was useless, but somebody had to stall things until Christian showed up, or he, Ed, and Magnus might be swinging from the gallows by the time the revolt started. He looked over his shoulder at the crowd, but saw no sign of Christian or his surprise.

Olympia rose up from her throne, towering on her highest heels, her purple velvet, ermine-trimmed cape billowing around her in the breeze, her diamonds flashing dazzlingly in the sunlight. The gapers took an awed breath in unison. The other subjects tightened their grips on their concealed weapons. "My opinion," she thundered, "is the only opinion that matters in this kingdom. How dare you question that? It only serves as further proof of your traitorous state of mind. *I* need no more proof than that. But because I am a fair and judicious ruler, a jury panel of three distinguished citizens will make the final judgment."

She continued to stand there, her cape billowing, her words ringing out over the crowd. A baby was crying somewhere, then was quickly silenced. Even Bub, Cate, Flopsy, Mopsy, and Topsy stopped fighting over the blue squeaky toy, which they had brought out into the bailey, and looked up at Olympia.

It seemed to all the rebels who had been going to great lengths to hide their weapons that this would be an excellent time for Christian to show up and start the revolt. They were armed, they were ready, they were eager—and they were so scared their mouths felt full of cotton.

"I declare this trial over," Olympia intoned into the hush. "Jury, what is your verdict?" She turned to three old men in long brown robes standing at the side of the platform.

"What?" said one.

"The trial's over?" said another.

"Wait," said the third. "I must have missed something."

Olympia's glare seemed capable of igniting them. "Remember what I told you," she hissed. "You are the jury—*my* jury—for this very important trial. The trial that will show all my subjects how judicious I am. And how futile and how dangerous it is to commit treason in this kingdom. Now, *what is your verdict?*" She lowered her voice. "And don't forget, there are sacks of gold coins waiting for you. There are also three gallows over there that can be used more than once."

"Oh," said the first old man. "Well, then, guilty, I guess."

"Me, too," said the second.

"Ditto," said the third.

Olympia faced the crowd again, her arms spread. "You've heard the verdict of the impartial jury. Rollo, ready the criminals for execution."

Rollo looked over his shoulder toward the drawbridge, but saw nothing coming. "Uh . . . ," he began. "I don't . . ."

Olympia's eyes narrowed. "Do you have a problem with my command, Rollo?"

"Uh, no, Your Majesty," Rollo said. "Absolutely

not." He poked Swithbert in the back with his sword, the tip of which was still bent. "Get moving," he ordered.

"Are you sure?" Swithbert whispered.

"No talking!" Rollo told him, and poked him again. "Grumley and Somerset, you bring the other two. Now!"

Marigold, in the shadows behind a pillar, put her hand over her mouth. Had Rollo betrayed them?

Grumley and Somerset (both looking confused) and Rollo marched the three prisoners to the gallows. "Up!" Rollo commanded, pushing Swithbert toward the steps. He beckoned to the masked hangmen. "Come get them." The hangmen descended the stairs, each one taking hold of a prisoner and escorting him to the top.

Marigold was frantic, racking her brain for a way to begin the revolution *now*, without Christian and the plan. Maybe she could start a distraction, a commotion—but what good would that do? None of the rebels would know what was happening. She cast a desperate glance around, looking for Susan, or Mr. Lucasa, or anybody who could help.

The hangmen were putting hoods over the heads of Ed, Magnus, and Swithbert, and then testing the strength of the ropes by yanking on them.

Marigold had no choice. She opened her mouth and let out a scream that could have shattered glass. If anyone had been able to hear it, that is. Completely obliterating her very proficient scream was a sound none of them had ever heard before—a loud, strange trumpeting sort of sound. It came from behind them. Before the crowd turned as one to see what was approaching, they observed the look on Olympia's face. It was so priceless that it delayed the turning around for a couple of seconds. Never before had they seen such an expression of disbelief, outrage, and fury on their queen. It was pretty impressive.

But then they turned—and there, coming under the portcullis, was an enormous white elephant. On his back was an old, old man in a ratty purple robe, and—could it be King Christian from Zandelphia dressed in his swankiest regal regalia, holding a strange instrument?

The elephant had its trunk in the air, trumpeting away, as if announcing its own arrival. The crowd quickly parted before the creature, which marched purposefully to Olympia's raised throne where, with one last blast from its trunk, it stopped. The crowd closed rank again behind the elephant (though directly behind an elephant is sometimes not the smartest place to stand) and waited expectantly.

"Who are you?" Olympia commanded. "What are you doing here?"

"You know me," Christian said. "Maybe you just don't recognize me with a crown on."

"I do know you," she said disdainfully. "And it takes more than a crown to impress me. Who is that with you? And what is this—this *animal*—for?"

"This is Wendell the wizard," Christian said. "And the animal is an elephant. It belongs to Wendell and its name is Hannibal. We thought this would be an imaginative way of announcing that you're in the middle of a popular revolt, starting right now. You have this opportunity to free Swithbert so that he can resume his throne, and to step down yourself. Or else you will be forced to do so."

"Forced by whom?" she asked, quite correctly.

"By your subjects." Christian gestured to the crowd around him. "Right?" he asked them.

Cheers erupted, with people waving their weapons in the air.

"Don't be absurd," Olympia thundered, ignoring the weapons, which irked the rebels and made them even more committed to the revolution. "You've interrupted a very important execution here."

"That was the idea," Chris said, loading a projectile into the miniature trebuchet he'd finally finished, and firing it over the heads of the crowd. It hit the upright post of the gallows Ed was standing in front of and broke the thing in two, rendering it useless. Two more projectiles shattered the other two gallows, and the next one broke the high carved back off the throne.

"You asked for it!" King Christian yelled, and blew the whistle around his neck.

# 33

After a moment of frozen shock, the masked executioners yelped and jumped off the platform. Ed, hooded and with his hands bound behind him, was yelping, too.

"What's happening?" he hollered. "What was that crash? Chris, has the fighting started? Somebody tell me something!"

"Be calm," Swithbert, equally bound and hooded, encouraged him. "I'm sure Chris and Marigold have everything under control. Has anybody else noticed how awful these hoods smell? I don't believe they've been washed in years. And they're *very* hot."

Magnus recognized that Swithbert was sounding a

bit delirious. Fear could do that, he knew, no matter how levelheaded one might normally be. "I agree, sire." Magnus spoke soothingly. "As soon as we have a chance, we must make sure they get laundered."

In the meantime, the noise around them—shouting, and screaming, and the elephant trumpeting—grew louder and more chaotic. Ed added to the noise by yelling, "What's happening? What's happening? What's happening?"

"Ed," Magnus said calmly, "I believe this is what a rebellion sounds like. As I'm sure you're aware, we are quite helpless as we are, so we must be patient and wait for someone to come help us. But they will, I'm sure they will."

Ed stopped yelling. "Magnus? Was that you? I thought you were the one who believes good luck is as scarce as a happy clam's teeth."

"Hmmm," Magnus mused. "You're right. I usually do feel like that." He raised his voice over the din around them. "But something changed when we were in the dungeon making plans. I *wanted* to believe things would work out. I *wanted* to believe I would survive, and that I could have the kind of life I've dreamed about. I figured that when there's no way of knowing what the future holds it's just as easy to believe it'll be good as to believe it'll be bad."

"What?" Ed yelled. "I can't hear over this noise!"

Magnus had to laugh. "Never mind. I'll tell you later."

"You're absolutely right," Swithbert said. "Good for you, Magnus. You know, I feel a little light-headed. I'd like to sit down."

Just as he began to sway, Lazy Susan and Mr. Lucasa were on either side of him, supporting him. Mr. Lucasa pulled the hood from his head. "Take a deep breath, sire," he told Swithbert as he eased him down to sit on the top step. "Susan, untie his hands, and then do the same for Ed and Magnus. They should see what's going on here."

The rebellious citizens had formed a ring around the platform where Olympia stood, and around the triple gallows scaffolding. They bristled with weapons—halberds and quarterstaffs, pitchforks and rakes—that kept anyone not with them at bay. Every now and then, one of the farmers would throw some of his produce—cabbages, rutabagas, broccoli—into the crowd. It was hard to tell who, if anyone, they were aiming at. Everyone yelled at the tops of their voices while they did whatever they were doing. Others rushed to get out of the way. As part of the plan to help separate the active rebels from the undecided and to boost support for Swithbert, Mr. Lucasa dipped into the shiny brass kettle he and Lazy Susan had carried into the bailey and began tossing out cookies decorated with Swithbert's face. The cookies were so good that some of the active rebels became distracted and lunged for them.

"No!" Lazy Susan screamed at them. "You know those aren't for you! And you know we have something even better waiting for you after this is over!"

Marigold and Lazy Susan darted through the crowd reassuring the spectators and the undecided that this uproar could be resolved if they would just stay calm and out of the way. In any other revolt, people would all probably have been scattering for the frontier, but they stayed put. For one thing, Lazy Susan and Marigold were so convincing and, for another, the spectators couldn't take their eyes off the great white elephant. Hannibal plowed through the crowd with Christian and Wendell on his back, Chris waving his little trebuchet encouragingly over the rioters' heads. Rollo stood before the queen, dodging vegetables, his sword pointed at the biggest diamond brooch on her bodice, while she screamed, "I'm the queen! Put that sword down!"

Rollo, who had straightened out the bent tip of his

sword, used it to snip one of the diamond buttons from the front of Olympia's dress. It rolled off the platform and into the crowd.

"Are you insane?" Olympia screamed, trying to lunge for the button, but prevented by Rollo's sword point.

"Get back where you were," he told her, "or I'll cut them all off."

She had no choice, but she sure didn't like it.

"And I'm one of the rebels," he said. "So I'm definitely not putting my sword down."

"What are you talking about? I saw you escort those traitors to the gallows."

"I would never have let those nooses be put around their necks. I was prepared to slay three executioners if I'd had to. I was just going along, waiting for the revolution to begin."

For once in her life, Olympia was speechless—but enraged nevertheless. Her face grew red and her mouth opened and closed, though only choked croaks and gasps came out.

When things seemed at a momentary lull—the traitors rescued, the queen and her supporters contained, and the rest of the populace munching cookies and watching the goings-on as if they were at a circus—Christian stood up on Hannibal's back and raised his arms. Once the din diminished, Christian spoke. "Everybody who wants to see a change in the rulership of Beaurivage is invited to join us in helping Olympia find another line of work. All of you, come over on this side, behind Rollo and his troops. Those of you who are satisfied with how your kingdom is being run under the current queen, or who remember what it was like before she went away, and want more of that, line up over there." He pointed to the other side of the courtyard. "Or we can fight and then you'll have to take what comes with whoever wins."

This is a dangerous moment in any revolt since the size of the divisions is unknown, as is the taste for violence. But fortune often favors the brave.

There was a period of uncertainty as the populace muttered among themselves about their loyalties, weighing the punishments for a failed revolt against those associated with plain old living under Olympia's rule. Some just wanted to be on the side of the good cookies. Then the people began shuffling around, choosing their alliances.

Christian was relieved that no one immediately chose more fighting. He'd taken seriously his promise to Marigold to limit the bloodshed.

When the shuffling stopped, there was a huge crowd behind Rollo and his guards, and a sparser but much more pugnacious-looking group on the other side of the bailey. As the groups stood glaring at each other a couple of peasants from the smaller group detached themselves and scuttled somewhat sheepishly over to join the larger group.

Chris pointed to the big crowd and addressed Olympia. "Your subjects have spoken. Are you ready to accept reality and go quietly?"

Her voice had returned and her outrage remained. "You're out of your mind. And will soon be back in the dungeon where you belong. Along with the rest of these—these—misguided citizens."

Marigold was sure she'd seen the word "boneheads" form on Olympia's lips before she said "misguided citizens."

There was some anxious murmuring in the big crowd. Even though they outnumbered Olympia substantially, her wrath was enough to make them feel their opposition was flimsy and unreliable.

Olympia, not one to miss any waffling, jumped right on their indecision. "I know none of you wants to make a stupid decision based on inadequate information," she said kindly. "So I'm going to give you this one chance to change your minds. For the next five minutes there will be amnesty, if you think you've made the wrong choice. No dungeons, no punishments. Anyone can make a mistake. What do you say?"

There was more anxious shuffling—made worse by the fact that the misguided citizens had no idea how long five minutes was. Wristwatches hadn't been invented yet, and sundials are better for hours than minutes. And then, only on a sunny day. Was five minutes a long time, or a short time? How long did they have to worry?

And whether they could trust Olympia to abide by her word was the bigger question. She had never received any medals for compassion. Could they believe her?

Marigold had run to Hannibal's side and called up to Chris, "Shouldn't you sit down? This elephant is very tall."

He grinned down at her. "Not yet. Presentation is important now. Olympia needs to see this revolt isn't just my idea, or yours, or even Swithbert's. The people need to show her how they feel and what they want. Come on up here with Wendell and me. You'll be safer. There's plenty of room and the view is great."

"But how—," Marigold began, just as Hannibal came down on his front knees, almost pitching Chris and Wendell off his back. "Oh," she said, climbing up onto one elephant knee and pulling herself the rest of the way with Hannibal's ear until Chris could drag her up.

"I wish he'd warn me before he does that," Wendell grumbled. "I don't always have time to grab onto the harness, and falling off him is a long way down."

Marigold clung to Chris. "A very long way down. That's what I was saying."

Sometimes—though not often—hesitation can be one's best friend. The five minutes passed while the dithering continued, and before the crowd knew the time was up, Olympia was bellowing at them again.

"I see! Well, never say I didn't give you a chance. You have only yourselves to blame for what's going to happen to you now." She turned her attention to the smaller group. "You, there! My loyal supporters who will be richly rewarded for your allegiance! Come to me!" And she beckoned with both bejeweled hands, the giant stones in her rings flashing in the sunlight.

The group, glancing suspiciously around, made its way as close to the platform as it could get, considering the ring of opposing guards around it. They stopped, gazing up at Olympia and the broken throne.

"Now," she said. "Attack them!" She pointed to the bigger crowd. "Drive them out of the castle."

The smaller group shifted uneasily until one of

them spoke up. "Um, Queen Olympia, we have no weapons. We were here for Market Day, not expecting a rebellion. And besides, they outnumber us ten to one or something like that. And they *are* armed. What do you suggest?"

"I suggest you *attack!*"

They simply stared back at her.

The bigger crowd looked on, caught between pity for the smaller group, astonishment and outrage at Olympia's continued imperiousness, and relief and amazement that, after so much anxious anticipation, it appeared the revolt could be accomplished fairly swiftly, and without bodily harm. It certainly helped to have been on the side with all the weapons.

But before anything else transpired, Hannibal stepped forward and reached out with his long trunk. He curled it around Olympia's waist and lifted her off her platform, appearing immune to her shrieks. Fenleigh, too, was making sounds no one had ever heard from him before.

"Hannibal! Stop!" Christian yelled.

"Stop, Hannibal!" Wendell repeated.

In fact, just about everybody (aside from a few supremely disgruntled subjects who were waiting eagerly to see just what Hannibal had in mind) was yelling to Hannibal to stop. But Hannibal apparently had his own plan.

He shook Olympia up and down so hard that her crown fell off, as did Fenleigh, who then scampered away through the crowd.

"Hannibal!" Wendell yelled. "Shaking won't work! She's really evil, not just unpleasant!"

"What are you talking about?" Chris asked, hanging on to both Marigold and Hannibal's harness, raising his voice over Olympia's screams.

"Hannibal thinks he can change people by shaking them. He thinks it rearranges what's inside their heads. But that only works for disagreeableness, not for true evil. In that case, the heart has to be rearranged, as well as the head. And nobody knows how to do that."

The crowd had retreated, away from the spectacle of Hannibal and Olympia, mesmerized and horrified at the same time.

Hannibal finally quit shaking the queen, but didn't let her go. She dangled from the grasp of his trunk, panting, wheezing, and still giving orders. "Put me down, you great stupid animal!"

Hannibal ignored her, as well as commands from Chris and Wendell, who were saying the same thing as

Olympia, but in much politer language. He seemed to be thinking.

Suddenly he lifted Olympia as high over his head as he could, and then let her go. She plummeted to the ground, her head hitting the cobblestones so hard the sound (the same sort of thunky splat a pumpkin might make) echoed off the castle walls. She lay still.

# 34

The crowd gasped, and then went completely silent, watching the queen, waiting for her to move.

She didn't.

Fenleigh came tearing out of the mob. He raced to Olympia and licked her face, making panicky whimpering noises. But still she didn't move.

"Where's the doctor?" Christian called from atop Hannibal. "Get him here. Have the queen taken to her bedroom." Then he realized that he shouldn't be the one giving directions now. This was not his kingdom. He motioned to Swithbert, who instantly understood.

King Swithbert rose, squared his shoulders, and quickly mounted the platform to stand in front of the ruin that had been his own throne. "The revolt is over," he told the crowd. "Queen Olympia is no longer in charge. The throne has been returned to its rightful monarch, and the constitution will be returned to its original state. Anyone who doesn't like that can register a protest on a form you can get at the guard office. Be sure to fill out the front *and* the back. Rollo, take the queen's supporters off to the dungeon for questioning."

While he was speaking, the court doctor and two helpers collected Olympia onto a stretcher and carried her away. The crowd gradually came out of its shock and the subjects began talking among themselves about the extraordinary things they had just witnessed. They kept a wide margin around Hannibal, even though he now seemed quite placid and relaxed.

Swithbert continued. "Now, please go on with your Market Day business while the quee—while Olympia is tended to. And somebody, bring this throne back into the throne room."

Slowly, the farmers and other vendors began picking up their knocked-over stands and gathering up their scattered goods, and the public began selecting items again. But it was definitely a Market Day they would not soon be forgetting.

Ed, Magnus, Lazy Susan, and Mr. Lucasa came

to stand beside Hannibal. Rollo and his guards rounded up the few of Olympia's supporters who had not melted off into the crowd, and who presumably wished that they had kept their loyalty to themselves—or perhaps not held it at all.

"Chris, how soon can we get down off this animal?" Marigold asked nervously.

"Can't get down off it," Ed called up to her, a twinkle in his eyes. "Down comes from ducks."

Marigold giggled, something she'd wondered this morning if she'd ever feel like doing again.

Christian looked at her fondly. When she was happy, so was he.

Wendell spoke a command to Hannibal, who knelt and allowed Chris and Marigold to slide off his back. Chris gave the elephant an affectionate pat.

"No," Marigold said to him.

"No? But I didn't say anything."

"I know that look on your face. And the answer is no. We do not need an elephant."

"Oh." He cast a wistful glance back at Hannibal. "I guess not. But he's lovely, isn't he?"

"I don't think I'd call him lovely. But he certainly came in handy."

"I guess we should go see how Olympia is,

shouldn't we?" Chris asked. "I had no idea Hannibal was going to do anything other than shake her. Wendell says he's never before done what he did to her."

"Maybe it's just what she needed, and Hannibal knew it," Marigold answered. "He might have more powers than Wendell. I hope it's taught her a lesson."

"But . . . I mean . . . she hit that ground pretty hard. I'm not sure she's still . . . I mean . . ."

Marigold waved a hand airily. "Don't worry. It'll take more than that to kill Olympia. She survived an underwater trip to Granolah on our wedding day, didn't she?"

"But . . . what if . . ."

"Who do you think will miss her if your *what if* is true?"

"Fenleigh?" Chris said. "Swithbert?"

"Papa didn't seem to miss her during the year she was gone. And I surely didn't. As for Fenleigh— maybe we could let him play with the dogs."

"The *dogs*? *Our* dogs? They hate Fenleigh. He used to chase them and nip at them and—"

"Oh, I know. But maybe it's their turn to—"

"Marigold! No! If we have to we'll find him another home. You wouldn't really turn him over to the dogs, would you?"

By this time they were on the staircase leading to Olympia's suite. "Oh, I guess not," she said. "But it's tempting, isn't it, to give somebody like Olympia or Fenleigh a taste of their own medicine? To get even?"

"I agree it's tempting. *Really* tempting. But it doesn't solve anything. It just perpetuates the problem by making us as bad as them. And we don't need any more of them, do we?"

Marigold pouted. "Oh, I know you're right. I just had a weak moment. You have to help me not do anything at all the way Olympia would."

"You could never be anything like Olympia. Don't worry. I know that no matter how many revenge thoughts you might have, you'd never act on them."

They entered Olympia's suite. Quite a few people were there already, including Mrs. Clover and Denby, milling around in the sitting room. They all stopped talking and turned when Marigold and Christian came in, followed by Ed and Magnus, who had come from Ed's suite, where they had gone to wash off their dungeon grime.

"How is she?" Marigold asked.

"The doctor's still in there," Denby said, "so we don't know yet. But you can go in. Seeing as who you are, I mean."

Much as she loved Zandelphia, sometimes Marigold forgot she was its queen and had the extra privileges that went with that. And sometimes, even when she did remember, she was reluctant to take advantage of her position. It just seemed unfair. But Christian was always ready to remind her that her position gave her heavy responsibilities as well, and that she had the power to do a lot of good, so she deserved a few treats.

"Right," Marigold said, and went to the bedroom door, pulling Chris along with her. She hesitated for a moment, and then opened the door, closing it behind them.

"Who *is* she?" Mrs. Clover whispered. "That filthy girl with King Christian?"

"Why, it's Queen Marigold," Denby said. "I don't know why she's so dirty unless it has something to do with the long-overdue rebellion."

"Oh, my," Mrs. Clover said, sitting down suddenly. "I didn't even recognize her. Wait until you hear what I did."

THE DOCTOR STOOD next to the bed, holding Olympia's wrist in one hand. He dropped it when he saw Christian, and bowed. "Your Highness," he said.

"She's a Highness, too," Chris said, indicating Marigold, "though hard to recognize right now. It's Queen Marigold."

The doctor's mouth fell open. "Oh" was all he could say.

"How is she?" Marigold asked.

"Well, she's alive," he said, recovering from his surprise, "but she's got a pretty big goose egg on the back of her head. And she hasn't woken up yet."

"But she will, won't she?"

The doctor shrugged. "I can't say. I've put leeches on her to bleed her, and we're washing her with cloths soaked in vinegar and honey—all the latest, most cutting-edge medical techniques. There's nothing more to be done. We just have to wait and see."

Marigold went to the bed where Olympia lay with her eyes closed, her hair disheveled, a bruise on her cheek, and Fenleigh crouched on the pillow. Marigold had expected, and even hoped, to feel a spasm of heart-deep pain for her. But all she experienced was the kind of human pity she would feel for any unfortunate person, underlain with the sense that Olympia had gotten what she deserved. As Ed would have said, what goes around, comes down like a ton of bricks.

"Well, keep us informed," she said to the doctor.

As she and Christian went down the corridor together, Chris said, "I know leeches are the standard treatment for just about everything, but it's such an odd idea, don't you think? How could it work?"

"Don't ask me. I'm not a doctor. But you're the inventor. Why don't you think up something better? Something a sick person could drink, or have put into them some other way if they're too sick, or too unconscious to swallow."

"That's a great idea! It makes much more sense to put something helpful *in* than to take something essential *out*. I'll work on it."

# 35

They found Swithbert in the throne room supervising the reinstallation of his throne, and consulting with the court carpenter about fixing the part the trebuchet had damaged.

"How is she?" he asked. Christian and Marigold told him what they knew, and then he dismissed the workmen. "Have a seat." He indicated the two side-by-side thrones that he and Olympia had once occupied. "I want to talk to you."

"There?" Chris asked, pointing to the damaged one. "That's your seat."

"I'll stand for a while," Swithbert said. "I've gotten over my light-headedness. Go ahead. Sit."

So Marigold and Christian sat in the thrones and waited.

Swithbert regarded them thoughtfully, and then spoke. "I've watched how you rule together and I've been impressed with your wisdom, your fairness, your prudence, and your real nobility. Nobility can sometimes be only a title, as it was with Olympia, and not a true condition of the heart and mind, as it is with both of you."

Marigold felt horribly guilty about even *thinking* of getting even with Olympia—and about what she'd suggested for Fenleigh. And grateful that her father saw her, as Olympia never had, in such a kindly way, overlooking her flaws.

"I think you are excellent rulers for Zandelphia. Beaurivage also needs excellent ruling, but I'm old and tired and I want to retire. We've talked about combining our two kingdoms before, and now I'd like to do it. Marigold would have been my natural successor if she'd remained Princess of Beaurivage, and if we make Beaurivage and Zandelphia one kingdom, she would still be the rightful queen of both parts of it. So what do you say?"

"Papa! You're not old and tired! I've seen you playing with the dogs. And sitting for hours at the snipsnapsnorum table with Ed. You still have lots of energy."

"Maybe so, precious. But now I want to spend it *all* on games with the dogs—and with Ed, too—and not on affairs of government. Besides, as I'm sure you've noticed, I'm not the best king. I've been too lax with my subjects and with Olympia. It's a wonder there hasn't been a revolution before now. One that aimed to depose *me*."

"Oh, sir," Christian said. "Your subjects love you. They would never do that."

Swithbert sighed. "They love me because they know they have nothing to fear from me. They know I'd never do anything to make things difficult for them, even if it would be for their own good. But they don't respect me." He hung his head.

Marigold and Christian were silent for a moment, recognizing the truth of what he'd said, but not wanting to agree.

Swithbert looked up. "I know many of them really disliked Olympia, but they may also have respected her because she was so strong in her point of view. They knew what to expect from her, even if it was nothing good. Does that make sense?"

"No, Papa," Marigold said. "It doesn't make sense. Look how your subjects rallied to you just today. No—" She held up her hand when he started to speak. "It wasn't just that they wanted Olympia gone. They want *you*."

"You're very kind to your old papa, precious. Really, I've had enough of the king business. I want to relax, and to sleep without worrying about my kingdom, and to have time to play with my grandchildren."

Marigold presumed he was referring to her sisters' children, but still, she looked at Christian and blushed.

"So, can you give me an answer? Soon?" Swithbert asked.

Christian reached between the two thrones to take Marigold's hand and said, "Yes, of course. Now maybe we should all go see about those supporters of Olympia's that Rollo has in the dungeon. We need to decide what to do with them."

"Quite so," Swithbert said, admiring Chris's decisiveness, and thinking that he was already a better king than he himself had been on his best day. "But can't we get Ed and Magnus and have some hoofenpoofer goulash first? All the uproar took my appetite for a while, but now I'm ravenous. And I know you all must be, too."

"You're right, Papa," Marigold said. "I'll race you to the kitchen."

# 36

Mr. Lucasa walked Lazy Susan back down to the scullery once it became clear that nothing would be happening soon with the ex-queen.

"What are you going to do now?" she asked him. "Since the rebellion wasn't a *yabu hebi ni naru*."

"You remembered that Japanese phrase for something backfiring!" he said, amazed. "Maybe you have a gift for languages, too. Well, since I'm not going to *taghairm,* I'll have to make my own decision." Seeing her eyebrows raised in question, he said, "The Scottish highlanders wrapped a man in a freshly butchered bullock's skin and took him to some wild and deserted place where the answer to his problem was supposed to be given to him by the spirits who live in such places. That's *taghairm*."

"Nice little word for a big idea," she said, thinking that maybe she *did* have a gift for languages. Maybe some *taghairm* would help her figure out what to do with it. But that part about the freshly butchered bullock's skin—she shuddered.

"I've been thinking about what I love most," Mr. Lucasa said. "I like to cook for people to the point of *slappare*—that's Italian for eating everything, right up to licking the plate—and I like to work hard making things more for the pleasure of it than the *lechuga*—Caribbean Spanish for dollars. I want to be *tubli*. That's Estonian for being orderly, and productive, and hardworking, and behaving properly. Being a good example."

"You want to do all that here?"

"I think I'd rather be self-employed than work for someone else. So I'll probably have to go somewhere else. And not back to my cottage. It feels too isolated after my time here among other people."

"Well, be careful what you call your new business. I heard about Wendolyn, this troll maiden who is Edric's girlfriend, who started her own travel service. She went out of business before long because, well, for one thing, nobody around here really travels for pleasure, and for another, she called her business Go Away. It makes sense, but it doesn't. Do you know what I mean?"

He chuckled and nodded.

"You have a nice laugh," she said. "You should laugh more often."

"Maybe I will. When I get my business started."

She looked down at her hands. "I'll miss you. You were part of my transformation, and I'll never forget that."

"Are you going to stay here? Working in the scullery?"

"I don't know. I've gotten so I don't mind working. In fact, I kind of like it. I've even decided I want to be called just Susan, without the 'lazy.' The name you've always called me. But I don't want to spend the rest of my life scrubbing pots. I'd like to do something more fun."

"Maybe you'd like to work for me. I have in mind what I want to do, but I'm going to need a lot of help."

"What? What are you going to do?"

So they sat down on a bench outside the kitchen door, and he took a long time telling her. When he finished, she said, "I can't think of anything I'd rather do more."

# 37

Once the occupants of the dungeon had been questioned, it seemed that most of them merely had misplaced loyalties and were easily convinced to abandon them, knowing that they would be under close scrutiny by Rollo for quite a while to make sure that they really had.

But there are always a few really bad apples who can influence others in an unfortunate direction. These have to be kept where they can do no further harm until it's known if they are willing to change their wicked ways and become productive members of society. Dungeons are a good place for them. But Marigold insisted to her father that they should eat something better than gruel. Making people eat gruel is not a good way to convince them to be nicer.

In the end only ten inmates remained in the dungeon. Christian, having had a lot of recent experience with how to get in and out, made sure all the escape routes were secured, and that the guards were changed on regular shifts. Thanks to Finbar, he knew the dangers of leaving one guard alone with prisoners for days on end.

As he was coming up the steps from the dungeon with Marigold and Swithbert, they became aware of a commotion.

"Not *again*," Swithbert said. "I've had enough commotions to last me the rest of my life." As he was saying this, he realized that he heard his own name amid the noise. He turned a frightened face to Chris and Marigold. "Do you think they're coming after me? For being such a bad king? They're saying, 'Where's Swithbert?'"

"Stay here," Chris said. "I'll go look. We can always get you out through the disposal tunnel if we have to." And he ran the rest of the way up the stairs. Within a minute he was back. "The doctor is looking for you. Olympia's awake."

Swithbert looked stunned. "I don't know why, but I thought it would take her a lot longer to wake up.

I should have known better. When it comes to Olympia, she does what she wants, when she wants." He squared his shoulders. "Well, let's go see her. She's not going to like hearing that the revolt is over and that she's out of a job."

As they appeared at the top of the dungeon stairs, someone spotted them and called, "There he is! The king!"

"Yes, yes," Swithbert said wearily. "Here I am."

The doctor met them outside Olympia's bedroom. "I can't explain what's happened," he said. "She's awake, but she's behaving strangely. Come on in. You'll see for yourself." He opened the door and ushered them in.

Olympia sat up in bed, the covers pulled to her chin, her eyes wide. Fenleigh still crouched on her pillow, and she cringed away from him, whimpering in what really did sound like fright.

"Olympia?" Swithbert said. "What's the matter? Are you in pain?"

"My head hurts," she moaned. "Can you take that animal away? He keeps trying to jump on me." Her voice ended in a wail of distress.

"Fenleigh? You don't want Fenleigh?"

"You know his name?"

Swithbert scratched his head. "Well, sure. He's

been yours since he was a pup. Or whatever baby weasels are called."

"Ferret, Papa," Marigold said. "Fenleigh's a ferret."

"Whatever," he said absently. "Anyway, you've never been afraid of him. And he's harmless—at least, as far as you're concerned. The rest of us are justified in being afraid of him. Look at those teeth."

"Just take him away. Please," Olympia wailed.

Gingerly, Christian picked up the squirming ferret while Marigold pulled the pillow slip from one of the many pillows on Olympia's bed. Together, they managed to get Fenleigh inside the pillow slip and to tie a knot at the top.

"There," Swithbert said. "All taken care of. What can we do for you now?" He expected her to say, "Give me the kingdom back." But what she said was, "You can tell me who you all are, and where I am, and what I'm doing here."

Christian, Marigold, and Swithbert looked at one another, and then back to her. "Why, Olympia," Swithbert said. "What do you mean?"

"Olympia?" she said. "Why are you calling me that? My name is Angelica. I live in Granolah. Is this Granolah?"

"Why, no." Swithbert looked over at Marigold and Christian, putting his finger to his lips and then making a twirling motion next to his ear. "You're in Beau-rivage. And I'm Swithbert, monarch of Beaurivage. This is my daughter Marigold, and her husband, Christian. Do you know any of us?"

She shook her head. "Ow! That makes my head hurt more. How did I get here? What happened to me?"

"Apparently you've hit your head. You should lie back and rest now. I think you have a friend here who can help explain things to you. Do you remember someone named Lazy Susan?"

"Of course. She's my best friend. But I prefer to call her just Susan. That word 'lazy' has such a nega-tive connotation, you know. She's here? Oh, I would love to see her. May I?"

No one had ever before heard Olympia ask per-mission for anything. Neither had they ever witnessed her trying to avoid hurting someone's feelings.

"We'll send someone for her right away," Swith-bert said. "We're going to leave you to rest now while we fetch her." He tiptoed out of the room, followed by Marigold and Christian, who held the squirming pillow slip.

Once they were in the sitting room, Chris handed the pillow slip to Denby. "Find somebody to figure out what to do with this ferret, will you please?"

"I think I'll just hang on to him for a while," Denby

said. He had already heard from Miranda, Olympia's maid, about her change of personality and name. "It seems cruel to separate him from—" He paused, not knowing how to refer to Olympia anymore. "From someone he's familiar with. I'm sure we can bring them together again."

"Good man, Denby," Chris said, clapping him on the shoulder. "Very compassionate."

Swithbert could hardly contain himself. He put his hands over his mouth to keep from crowing, but he was jumping up and down with excitement. When he was calmer, he said in a loud whisper, "Her amnesia is back! She's not Olympia anymore!"

"We gathered that, Papa," Marigold said. "And Angelica seems just the way Lazy Susan—I mean, Susan—described her, so I don't think she's faking. But what are we going to do with her? What if she loses her amnesia like she did before? She's still a problem."

"Marigold! She thinks she lives in Granolah. We can send her back there with La—I mean, with Susan. She was happy there. Maybe that's where she's meant to live."

Marigold threw a desperate look at Chris. "Talk to him, Chris," she implored. "We can't just make her somebody else's problem. We have to solve her."

"She's right, Swithbert," Chris said. "We have to find a real solution. It's tempting, I know, to palm her off on someone else, but she's ours. Like it or not."

Just then, Sedgewick, the head butler, came in with Lazy Susan and Mr. Lucasa, both of whom looked apprehensive. Susan gave Marigold, still in her filthy dress, an odd look.

"Swithbert said there was news about Olympia," Susan said. "What does he mean? Oh." She curtsied to Swithbert. "Your Highness. Sire."

"Apparently that bump on the head from being dropped by Hannibal made her lose her memory again," Swithbert told her. "The way she did when she showed up in Granolah. Maybe she hit her head on a rock while she was in the river that time."

"Very possible," Susan said. "Are you saying she's changed from Olympia to Angelica again? Can you tell the difference?"

"*Can* I?" Swithbert said. "She's a completely different person. A nicer one. Is that how Angelica was in Granolah?"

"Oh, yes. Angie was lovely. Gentle and funny and sweet."

"Hard to believe," Swithbert muttered.

"I know," Susan said. "When she turned back into Olympia, I thought she was playing some kind of joke.

Not a very funny one, either." She gave Marigold another odd look.

"Hi," Marigold said. "I know you think my name is Mary and that I'm a maid, but my real name is Marigold. From Zandelphia. I'm the queen there. Thanks for your help with the rebellion."

Susan took a step back and put her hand on Mr. Lucasa's arm for support.

"I know, I know," Marigold said, indicating her dress. "This is a disguise. I apologize for not telling you when we were in the scullery together—no, no, please don't curtsy. When you've scrubbed kettles with someone that seems rather silly. Anyway, in the scullery I had to protect our plan for the uprising, and I didn't know yet who I could trust. So please forgive me. Now, about Olympia. The fact that Angie's shown up—and she's just the way you said she was—don't you think this means that she had a nice person in her all the time, but just hidden?"

"I don't know what it means," Susan said. "Your Highness. Ma'am." She'd thought it was strange the way Mary—Marigold—had taken charge of calming the crowd at the rebellion, but she'd figured people did unexpected things in a crisis. "It's like she's two separate people stuck together. Not like she's two kinds of people *mixed* together. There's nothing of Olympia in Angelica, and vice versa."

"So, the one we want to keep is Angelica," Marigold said. "We just have to make sure Olympia never comes back."

"Do you know how to do that, Your Highness?" Mr. Lucasa put in. "Because it's the only solution. I've never known her as Angelica, only as Queen Olympia, and only for a short time, but already she's made me *mukamuka.*"

"I'm sorry?" Marigold said. "Did you say *mukamuka?*"

"Yes, Your Highness. It's Japanese. It means feeling so angry you want to throw up."

"What a great word!" Marigold exclaimed. "I wish I'd known it when I was growing up. She made me feel like that almost every day. Excuse me, but I don't know who you are."

He bowed, doffing the chef's toque he was wearing. "Stan Lucasa, Your Highness. Queen Olympia stopped at my house for food on the way to Beaurivage and brought me along with her, to be her chef and her dressmaker."

"Interesting combination," Marigold said.

"I like creating things. And I like helping people,

and making them happy. But I have to say, the queen was a hard woman to please. Or—excuse me for saying so—to like. Especially after she told me how much she enjoyed fox hunting."

"You're telling me. I hate even the idea of fox hunting." Marigold turned to Susan. "She's pretty upset now. I mean, Angelica is. And she really wants to see you."

"All right." Susan sounded apprehensive.

Swithbert opened the bedroom door. Angelica held out her arms to Susan and burst into tears. Susan rushed into the room and Swithbert closed the door behind her.

"If you'll pardon me, Your Highnesses," Mr. Lucasa said to Swithbert, Chris, and Marigold, "I might have some help for your situation."

"Please go on," Swithbert said. "We'll listen to any suggestion, no matter how bizarre."

"It's not *too* bizarre," Mr. Lucasa said.

Swithbert motioned them all to chairs in the sitting room. Mr. Lucasa waited for the monarchs to sit before he did.

"I've been talking to Wendell, the wizard who owns that magnificent elephant. And, by the way, I don't think the elephant is a threat to anyone besides Olympia. He has a finely developed sense of justice, and he dispenses it as he sees fit. I was admiring him while Wendell calmed him down after the . . . the incident. I must say, I do have high regard for a man with an impressive means of transportation. And I discussed something interesting with Wendell that might be of help to us. About getting rid of Olympia."

Marigold interrupted. "I've already spoken to him about that. He can only do immobilizations, vaporizations, and explosions. And vaporizations of evil people—as I believe Olympia is—leave behind bad energy that keeps working. The only way to cure evil people is by rearranging their heads and hearts, and nobody knows how to do that."

"I think Hannibal does," Mr. Lucasa said. "I think that's what he was trying to do when he shook her, and then dropped her. And maybe it worked. At least partially. To finish the job, I believe Wendell and I can do a vaporization spell on only the part that's Olympia. And I don't think it will harm the part that's Angelica because they're completely separate people."

"But what if it does?" Swithbert said. "That would be terrible. Harming an innocent person."

"Wendell doesn't have the best reputation for success," Marigold said gently. "And we know nothing about your magical skills. What makes you think you can do something this hard?"

"Wendell says since he's been at your castle in Zandelphia, he's been getting enough sleep and enough to eat, which he hasn't had for years, and he's had a lot of time to experiment with things. So he's gotten better at magic."

"Maybe he has," Christian said to Marigold. "I suppose it's possible."

"Go on, Mr. Lucasa," Swithbert said. "Tell us what you can do."

"I've lived alone for a long time, in a part of the country where a lot of travelers passed by my cottage. I like to cook, so occasionally one of them would come in for a meal—and sometimes end up staying for days."

"Say," Swithbert said. "Did you make me boiled eggs for breakfast *and* lunch one day?"

"Indeed I did."

"Then I can understand why they wanted to stay. Best eggs I ever ate."

"Thank you. Well, I met some interesting people that way, and I learned something from almost every one of them. Including that spell. I confess I've never had to try it, but I have the recipe with me, and Wendell has all the equipment and ingredients we'll need. We're pretty confident we can vaporize Olympia without harming Angelica."

"But what about the bad energy Olympia would leave behind?" Marigold asked. "That would be almost as bad as still having her here."

"I think this is the best time to do it, while her heart and mind are still all shaken up by Hannibal. Before her substances settle back to the way they were."

There was a long silence.

"Did you have some other solution in mind?" Mr. Lucasa asked finally. "Something you think would work better?"

After another long silence, Swithbert said, "No."

Chris, seeing how reluctant Swithbert was, as always, to make a decision that might turn out poorly for someone, acted like a king and spoke. "I know we'd be taking a risk for Angelica, but if we really want Olympia gone for good, this may be the only way. What would you say about asking Angelica how she'd feel about it?"

More long silence. Marigold went to sit beside her father and held his hand. "Olympia's given you nothing but trouble for years, Papa. And she was willing to eliminate you, and Ed, and Magnus to get what she wanted. Not to mention what she wanted to do to you and me before I married Chris just so she could be the sole ruler. She's evil, Papa. Truly."

He sighed and squeezed her hand. "I know. I do know."

"I understand," Mr. Lucasa said, "how difficult a decision this is. But you don't want to be *a'anu* forever, do you? It's a Cook Island word meaning to sit all huddled up, pinched and miserable. And it seems to me she's made almost her whole kingdom feel that way. It's not good leadership."

Swithbert sighed again, and said, "All right. Let's go talk it over with Angelica."

# 38

Angie had been calmed considerably by Susan's presence (and Fenleigh's absence), and listened to all they had to say without interruption—something Olympia would have been incapable of doing. As Mr. Lucasa said, Olympia was very good at *nyelonong*—Indonesian for interrupting without apology.

When they had finished telling Angie about the possibility of separating her from Olympia permanently, she sat clutching Susan's hands in both of hers, clearly frightened. "This Olympia sounds like a terrible person. I hate the idea that she's part of me."

"She isn't, actually," Mr. Lucasa said. "She's separate from you. Just sharing your living quarters, let us say. What we want to do is evict an unwanted tenant. An irresponsible, destructive one. One, say, with a long *accordéon*, which is French for an extensive criminal record."

"When you put it that way," Angie said, "it makes me want her out of here right now. Except for what could happen to me in the process." Her lower lip began to quiver.

Swithbert, Marigold, and Christian watched it, amazed. She looked exactly like Olympia, but behaved so unlike her that it was positively disorienting.

"I suggest we get Wendell up here immediately," Mr. Lucasa said. "We can't waste any time. That bad energy could be settling itself while we speak."

"Of course," Swithbert said. "I'll send Denby for him."

WITHIN A FEW MINUTES, Wendell was there, carrying his bag of wizardry ingredients, bowing over and over again. Never before had he been in the presence of so much royalty, and it was making him pretty nervous.

"Wendell," Marigold said, "would you like a moment to collect yourself and get prepared?" The idea of a twitchy wizard with a poor record of successes attempting a tricky spell was making her feel the need to collect herself as well.

"Good idea. Yes, indeed." He mopped his brow with his sleeve.

After a few minutes in the dressing room with Mr. Lucasa, reviewing the process, while the others paced anxiously and Angie lay, ashen, on her pillows, Wendell and Mr. Lucasa returned, smiling and apparently confident.

Angie sat up. "What should I do?" she asked in a trembling voice.

"We need some items from you," Mr. Lucasa said. "Things that only Olympia would have touched. Nothing that you've had contact with since you became Angie again."

"That would be almost everything she owned, since I've been Angie for only a few hours. But take it. Take it all. Gowns, furs, jewels, whatever you can find. I don't want any of it enough to be her again."

Swithbert winced watching Mr. Lucasa go through the drawers of Olympia's jewelry chest. Nothing in there had cost him less than—well, he wouldn't want to say, but a *very* great deal—and he would hate to see so much of an investment be melted, or whatever was going to happen to it. But on reconsideration, he decided he agreed with Angie—he didn't want any of it enough to get Olympia back. "Take it all," he encouraged Mr. Lucasa.

"This is just what I need." Mr. Lucasa picked up a handful of tortoiseshell hairpins. He held them in front of Angie. "Now, breathe on them. Don't touch them, just breathe." Angie huffed a little puff of air onto the hairpins. "Now spit on them."

"Really?" Angie said. "I mean . . . your hand . . ."

"It's all right," he said. "I'm washable."

"Are you sure about this?" Wendell asked. "I've never seen such a thing."

"It's in the recipe," Mr. Lucasa said. "There are times when one can improvise with a recipe, but this is not one of them. Now lie back and close your eyes."

Angie fell back onto the pillows with a thump and squeezed her eyes shut, as if expecting a blow.

Mr. Lucasa, humming softly, set a stone bowl on the bedside table and began asking Wendell for items. "One tablespoon slime mold, half a cup of wrack, pinch of Venus flytrap. Thank you. Two grams figwort, one of deadly nightshade, dash of bittersweet. Thank you. Now the hairpins, three shakes powdered cankerworm, and a third of a cup of slivered snout beetle. That's it."

"They *do* seem to know what they're doing," Marigold whispered to Christian. He patted her hand and held his breath.

Mr. Lucasa stopped humming and began muttering as he crushed the ingredients in the bowl with a big stone pestle. Wendell muttered along with him, reading his lines from the recipe card. A strong odor was released—part sweet, part rotten, part spicy. "Like most people," Wendell commented, while the others held their noses, and Angie squinched her eyes more tightly closed.

A dark purple cloud rose above the stone bowl and swirled like a little tornado. It meandered about the room indecisively and then stopped, as if gathering strength. After a moment, it tore across the room like a purple arrow, straight for Angelica.

Marigold gripped Christian's arm so hard he winced.

The purple arrow went straight into Angie's right ear and disappeared. Everyone gasped at once as Angie began to thrash and writhe on the bed.

Swithbert covered his eyes with his hands. Susan covered her mouth with her hands. Mr. Lucasa covered his ears with his hands. Marigold clutched Christian hard enough to leave bruises. And Wendell's mutterings changed to whimperings. "Oh, dear. Oh, dear. Oh, dear," he moaned.

The battle inside Angie went on for several minutes. Then suddenly she was still. Totally, utterly still. A pale lavender vapor leaked out of her ear and lay on the pillow, a misty smudge. All that remained of the odor was a faint sweetness.

Susan was the first to move, taking Angie's limp hand in her own. "Angie, dear," she whispered. "Are you there?"

No answer.

Susan put her arms around Angie, tears welling in her eyes. "You were the bravest person I knew," she said, weeping.

Angie coughed, and Susan sat up. "Angie?"

"Huh?" Angie opened her eyes. "What happened? I feel so strange. As if I'd been turned inside out or something."

"Wait," Swithbert said. "You *are* Angie, right? You wouldn't answer to the name Olympia if I called you that, would you?"

"No," Angie said, and coughed again. "Because that's not my name."

"What about me? What's my name?"

She started to speak, and then frowned. "I guess I

never heard it. I'm sorry. We were never actually introduced."

Still not convinced, he stepped over to the jewelry chest and took up a handful of sparkling baubles. Carrying them to the open window, he said, "What would you say if I were to drop these out the window?"

"I would hate to see such valuable things thrown away, but they're not mine. I can't tell you what to do with them."

"She's Angie, all right," Swithbert crowed. "Olympia would have been out of that bed in a flash, saving the jewelry and dropping *me* out the window!"

Mr. Lucasa stepped up to Wendell and shook his hand. "We did it! We actually did it! I don't know how much call there is for that kind of a spell, but you really nailed it. I feel like giving you a present. How would you like a new robe? That one's definitely seen better days."

Wendell tottered weakly and held on to Mr. Lucasa. "It really did work, didn't it? To tell you the truth, I was pretty sure we couldn't do it."

That wasn't exactly what Marigold would have preferred to hear, but it didn't matter now. The spell had vaporized Olympia.

Wendell recovered himself and went to examine

the pale lavender stain on the pillow. "I thought there'd be more left," he said. "But Olympia fought like a tiger. There was just barely enough."

"Where—," Swithbert began, "where is she now? Do you know?"

"I don't," Wendell said. "But it's somewhere she can't come back from, we're sure of that. I just hope we acted in time, and there isn't any negative energy left behind."

As he said that, the big gold-framed mirror over the vanity table cracked right down the middle, releasing a little puff of lavender smoke.

"Oooh!" they all said, as a shiver went up their spines.

"I guess .here is," Wendell whispered. "But maybe that was the last of it."

At that, a picture on the wall next to the door fell off its hook and hit the floor with a crash, breaking its frame.

"I should have known she wouldn't go quietly," Swithbert said.

"But she *is* going, right?" Marigold asked.

"Oh, she's going, all right," Mr. Lucasa said. "She's *gone*. But I'm afraid we weren't quite in time to vaporize *all* her bad energy. At least it's not in Angie, but some of it got left behind in the atmosphere. So just remember that. If you're having a rough spot and feel extra cross and critical, that's probably just leftovers from Olympia getting in your head and making you behave badly."

"What should we do to stop it?" Christian asked.

"You should work extra hard to be your best selves. True evil has a hard time operating in the face of strenuous manifestations of good. Especially if you act right away. The longer you let evil hang around and get a grip on you, the harder it is to get rid of it."

"Yes, I know." Swithbert sighed, thinking of all the years with Olympia.

"You never acted evilly, Papa," Marigold said, consoling him.

"I never acted at all," he said. "I was weak."

"Evil can do that to you, too," Wendell said, packing up his bowl and pestle and the leftover ingredients. "Scare you into inaction."

"Is there something I can take? Some powder or elixir that will give me strength against it?"

Wendell shook his head. "Not that I know of. The only antidote to evil I've ever heard of is what Mr. Lucasa told you—just to be as actively good as you can be in the face of it. Now, about my fee—"

"It's not going to be a firstborn child," Marigold said, stepping in. "I can tell you that right now. And not an arm and a leg, either."

Wendell shook his head. "I wasn't even going to ask."

"Come with me," Swithbert said. "We can discuss terms." He took Wendell by the arm with one hand and guided Mr. Lucasa with the other, and they went out into the sitting room.

Marigold turned back to Angie. "Still feeling all right?" she asked.

"Just fine," Angie said, fussing with her hair—always a sure sign that someone is improving. "I suppose I should start thinking about what I'll be doing next. I think it would be a mistake for me to hang around here looking like the queen everybody disliked so much."

"You could go back to Granolah," Chris said. "I hear you liked it there."

She turned to Susan. "We could do that."

"Oh," Susan said. "I'm . . . I'm not going back to Granolah. I'm going into business with Mr. Lucasa. But you could come with us. We're going to need lots of help."

"You're going into business? But you never liked working when I knew you in Granolah."

"Well, that's changed. I'm not *gorogoro* anymore."

"*Gorogoro?*"

"It's Japanese for lying around doing nothing. I'm learning languages from Mr. Lucasa. In our new business, it will be an advantage to speak as many as we can."

"What is this new business?" Angie asked.

Susan looked around. "It's still sort of a secret."

Chris took Marigold by the arm. "We were just leaving," he said. And they did.

# 39

They strolled along the terrace that had been the scene of so much drama during their acquaintance: where they had first communicated by p-mail, where Marigold had saved Christian's life, where they were married, where Olympia had fallen into the river.

"A lot has happened to us on this terrace," Chris said.

"I was just thinking that," Marigold said. "This seems like a good place to make another big important decision."

"Perhaps you're right," Chris said. "Do you want to be queen of Beaurivage *and* Zandelphia?"

"I have a lot of unhappy memories of Beaurivage. Maybe coming back and correcting some of the sad things would be good for me."

"Olympia's gone. That's one big correction. But I wouldn't want you to do something you don't feel right about." He took her into his arms. "I already feel terrible about every little thing I've ever done that's made you sad."

"I've been thinking about that, too," she said, resting her head on his chest. "I'm starting to believe that happily ever after includes people doing things that upset each other. We all get cranky, or impatient, or worried, or careless enough to do or say things that hurt someone else. Like it or not, that's normal. We can't blame it all on Olympia's bad energy. The important part is that we feel sorry about what we've done and make up for it. That's something Olympia never did."

"That makes perfect sense. You were brilliant to think of it." Chris had begun to figure out that most people got way more criticism than praise, and that any bit of praise that could honestly be given, should be. Especially to a loved one. "I'll go along with whatever you want to do. Because I want what makes you happy. If you're happy, I am, too."

Marigold raised her head and looked at him. "I think we'll make perfectly splendid rulers of Zandelphia-Beaurivage."

He kissed her with his whole heart, and it was as glorious a kiss as the first one they'd ever shared.

# 40

Swithbert, Mr. Lucasa, and Wendell negotiated a decent price for the vaporization of Olympia, and in the process Swithbert discovered that Wendell had accumulated master points in snipsnapsnorum.

"Is that because you use magic?" Swithbert asked. "I cheat, but I'd be open to learning something even more helpful."

"No magic is allowed in any card game," Wendell said sternly. "Only cheating."

"Then would you be interested in joining Ed and me in some play?" Swithbert asked. "We'd welcome some new blood at our table. And if Chris and Marigold accept my offer to combine our kingdoms,

I'd like to start running snipsnapsnorum tournaments in my retirement. I want to do something lots more fun than ruling a kingdom. Maybe you'd be interested in helping with that."

"I suppose I could stay on." Wendell restrained himself from jumping up and down. "I have no other immediate commitments." He actually had none at all, and had been wondering what he would do with himself as wizardry technology passed him by, leaving him fussing with lungwort and salamander eyes and chicken feet while the younger wizards had moved on to runes and telepathy, snake stones and divining rods.

He'd never been very good at wizardry anyway, but he'd been pushed into it by his father, who had been something of a legend in his time. It's always hard to follow in the footsteps of a legend, especially when you don't even want to. What Wendell really loved was working with animals, which was why he and Hannibal got along so well. The vaporization spell had used up everything he had—he could feel that—and its success he could only call a miracle, which he actually thought he believed in more than magic. But he was done now, and he knew it. As ready for retirement as Swithbert was.

"You don't mind having an elephant as a guest?" he asked Swithbert.

"Not at all. I'm a great animal lover myself. I'll have to introduce you to my unicorn, Razi. And I saw how Christian looked at your beast. He'd love having him around for as long as you want to stay. Now, what do you say we go downstairs and get ourselves one of those nice big desserts Mr. Lucasa made for the rebels, and dig up Ed for some snipsnapsnorum?"

"It would be my great pleasure."

# 41

Magnus wept with relief at finally being back in his own beautiful house. He took a long, hot bubble bath, and dressed at last in clean clothes. Then, remembering how it felt to think he was close to extinction, he vowed not to waste a single moment of every precious day he had. He had to see Sephronia. Right now. In his fanciest coach with his pranciest horses. He was going to convince her that she had to marry him, the sooner the better. And he wasn't going to take no for an answer.

Sometimes, he was beginning to understand, you had to give what you wanted a pretty big push so it would fall into your lap.

———

SEPHRONIA SAT at her harp plinking on the strings while tears ran down her cheeks. She was overjoyed that Magnus hadn't been executed, but she missed him so much it hurt in her stomach and in her head. She couldn't even remember exactly what had made her so sure he wasn't interested in her anymore. She hadn't been able to explain it to her puzzled parents the very night it happened, either.

As she plinked and wept, through the French windows of the music room she could see a fancy carriage coming up the curving drive, pulled by a pair of prancing horses. She stood up to get a closer look. Could that be Magnus driving?

She ran to the door and was waiting when Magnus stopped the coach and jumped down from the driver's seat.

"Sephronia!" he called, waving a letter he had written to her in the dungeon. "I love you!" His declaration came out somewhat more suddenly than he'd planned, but it had the desired effect. Sephronia ran across the drive into his arms.

There are times when a personal visit is ever so much more effective than even the best letter or p-mail.

# 42

Susan, Mr. Lucasa, and Angie sat in Olympia's sitting room discussing plans for the new business.

"I'll have to sell my cottage," Mr. Lucasa was saying, "and the workshop will take some time to build, but while that's happening, we can hire the workers—Ed can help with that, I'm sure—and finalize all the details."

"We're going to need a lot of space and seclusion," Susan said, "so I think we should go somewhere far away."

"I have a place in mind," Mr. Lucasa said, "on the top of the world. Doesn't that sound like the perfect place from which to oversee everything we're planning?"

"I'll do my best to be a great project manager," Angie said. "Apparently as Olympia I didn't do much that was helpful, but in Granolah I learned a lot about managing. I lived with the mayor, after all."

"If you're willing to work, you can learn to do about anything," Susan said. "And those are words I never expected to hear coming out of my own mouth." She laughed. "Now, the last thing we have to do is find a name for our business. Since it's all Mr. Lucasa's idea, I think it should be named for him. I've been fiddling around making anagrams out of his name, and I think I've come up with something. It just needs a little tinkering."

She put a piece of paper in front of them. Written across the top was STAN LUCASA, and underneath were all the combinations of letters she'd been able to think of, none of which made any sense at all, including:

ASA CALNUTS
SAL NATSUCA
SALSA CATUN
LASSA TUNAC
LUTS SAANAC

At the very bottom of the page was a name with a circle around it. "This is the one I think we should use," Susan said. "I can't explain why—it just seems right. What do you think?"

"Santa Claus," Mr. Lucasa said slowly, trying it out. "Santa Claus. I like it. I like it a lot. It reminds me a little of the Zambian word for laughing without reason. Or the Indonesian one for the nine basic commodities needed for everyday life. In case you're interested, they're rice, flour, eggs, salt, sugar, cooking oil, kerosene, dried fish, and textiles. I think toys should be the tenth. It's also similar to the Malay word for the span between the tips of the outstretched thumb and little finger, for what that's worth. Thank you, Susan. It's perfect."

She beamed, and that smile of pure pleasure from a job well done made her look every bit as beautiful as her half sister—a fact that was not for one second wasted on Mr. Santa Claus, who was thinking that one more thing his new business needed was a Mrs. Santa Claus.

"I'm so happy to have you both as my companions in this endeavor," he said. "We have a lot of hard work ahead of us, but I think this enterprise will bring joy to many children. At the same time we'll be privileged to have jobs that feed our senses and our souls, which the best jobs do. What could be better? Now, before we get started on all we have to do, I want to make sure that I've made enough of those blue squeaky toys to leave behind so that the dogs never have to fight over one again."

# 43

Ed encountered Swithbert and Wendell in the corridor on the way to the game room.

"Come with us, Ed," Swithbert said. "We can play some three-handed snipsnapsnorum and get even more in debt to each other. Wendell cheats, too, but he swears he won't use any magic. And then we're going to figure out how to set up some tournaments so we can get to know other players. We'll have to think up a catchy name for the tournaments. In my mind I've just been calling them the X-Games. And I think Finbar has just the persuasive qualities we need to promote them."

"You two start without me," Ed said. "I've decided

I've got to cut to the cheese with Wendolyn, even if I do it like a bowl in a china shop. I'm not wasting any more time. If Olympia had had her way, I could be iced now, and never gotten another chance to ask Wendolyn to marry me. And whether or not she says yes, I'm getting Magnus to design me a new house that looks like my old crystal cave. I really do want Marigold and Chris to keep the original one, especially now that they've done all that remodeling, but I want one of my own, too. I can run Tooth Troll Limited just as well from there as from here. Once I get all that taken care of, we can go at this tournament business hammer and thongs. Wish me luck. Next time you see me, I'll either be in eighth heaven, or feeling like I've got ham and eggs on my face."

"Good luck, Ed," Swithbert said, watching him go. To Wendell, he said, "Have you ever been married?"

"No. Hannibal has been my sole companion these many years. I've moved around too much to put down any roots."

"Well, now that you'll be staying here, perhaps you'll find a suitable match. I have no objection to romance in spite of my own experience. Not at all. My daughters, as well as many others, have been quite fortunate in that area. And some, such as I—not so lucky. Come to think of it, Mrs. Clover has been a widow for a good long time. Perhaps one or the other of us should give her a closer look."

"Maybe the winner of our first hand should be the one to have the first chance," Wendell said, as Swithbert drew him into the game room.

They both were thinking about how to use their most extravagant cheating techniques.

# 44

We should go home," Marigold said, leaning on the parapet of the terrace, looking across the river to Zandelphia. "We need to check up on how things are going since we've been so preoccupied with Beaurivage."

"All right," Chris replied. "But first I have a knock-knock joke for you."

"Really?" Marigold exclaimed, clapping her hands. "I'm so glad you find them as interesting and as much fun as I do. Go ahead. I'm ready."

"Knock, knock."

"Who's there?"

"Dewey."

"Dewey who?"

"Dewey have to keep telling knock-knock jokes?"

"Dewey have to—," she repeated, and then got it. "You mean you don't like them after all?"

"I'm afraid that's what I do mean." Chris took her hands. "But I know how you love them, and I don't want to deprive you of the pleasure of them. So, how about you tell them to anyone you like. Except me. You can establish a Knock-Knock Joke Society and give a prize for the best one, or an Academy for the Promotion of Knock-Knock Jokes, or whatever you like. I'd just prefer never to hear another one as long as I live."

Marigold frowned. She wanted him to like those jokes as much as she did. She wanted him to like *everything* exactly as much as she did. She wanted to share every thought in her head with him. But he was Christian, not Marigold. He had his own thoughts and preferences. The fact that he wasn't exactly like her was what made him interesting. And annoying, and exasperating, and vexing—and adorable.

The silence was going on a little too long for Christian, and he was starting to think he should have kept his mouth shut and just put up with the knock-knock jokes, no matter how irksome they were. Maybe he'd started trouble when he shouldn't have, and they would begin to pick at each other again. It would be handy to have the excuse of Olympia's lingering bad energy for any such behavior, but Marigold had convinced him that such things were just what happened when two people were close, and wanted to be.

He was about to tell her to forget he'd said anything at all, when she said, "Could you stand to hear just one more?"

Relieved, he said, "Sure. Lay it on me."

"Knock, knock."

"Who's there?"

"Olive."

"Olive who?"

"Olive you."

"Olive . . . *ooh*. I love you, too," he said, figuring it out. "You can tell me that one any time you like." He folded her into his arms.

AND THEY lived happily (aside from a few normal disagreements, misunderstandings, pouts, silent treatments, and unexpected calamities) ever after.

Acclaim for ONCE UPON A MARIGOLD:

"Readers will gobble this story up."
—*VOYA*

"Great fun."
—*SLJ*

"Winning characters, unabashedly lame jokes, and a fresh,
energetic telling that will appeal to boys and girls alike."
—*Booklist*

An ALA Notable Children's Book
An ALA Best Book for Young Adults
A Smithsonian Magazine Notable Book
A VOYA Teens' Top Ten Book
A Junior Library Guild Selection
A New York Public Library 100 Titles for
Reading and Sharing Selection

www.jeanferris.com